P9-CNI-387

TARYN SOUDERS

Sky Pony Press
New York

Copyright © 2015 by Taryn Souders

All rights reserved. No part of this book may be reproduced in any manner without the express written consent of the publisher, except in the case of brief excerpts in critical reviews or articles. All inquiries should be addressed to Sky Pony Press, 307 West 36th Street, 11th Floor, New York, NY 10018.

Sky Pony Press books may be purchased in bulk at special discounts for sales promotion, corporate gifts, fund-raising, or educational purposes. Special editions can also be created to specifications. For details, contact the Special Sales Department, Sky Pony Press, 307 West 36th Street, 11th Floor, New York, NY 10018 or info@skyhorsepublishing.com.

This is a work of fiction. Names, characters, places, and incidents are either the products of the author's imagination or used fictitiously.

Dictionary definitions found at the beginning of each chapter come from either the *Oxford American Dictionary* or *Merriam Webster*.

Sky Pony® is a registered trademark of Skyhorse Publishing, Inc.®, a Delaware corporation.

Visit our website at www.skyponypress.com.

10 9 8 7 6 5 4 3 2 1

Library of Congress Cataloging-in-Publication Data is available on file.

Cover design and illustrations by Chris Piascik

Print ISBN: 978-1-63450-162-0
Ebook ISBN: 978-1-63450-927-5

Printed in the United States of America

TO ELLA HUNTER AND ANYONE WHO HAS EVER
WISHED THAT SPIDERS AND MATHEMATICS
WEREN'T A PART OF REAL LIFE.

CONTENTS

CHAPTER ONE

LUCK

luck

noun \luk\

—a force that brings good fortune or adversity
—the events or circumstances that operate for
or against an individual

The pouring rain the night before clued me in—misfortune was fast approaching.

The last three times we had a spring storm, awful things happened right after. First, while Dad was trying to repair a leak, he slipped off the roof and broke his leg. Next, Mom made meatloaf for dinner, which would have been bad enough—I detest meatloaf—even if we all hadn't gotten food poisoning the very next day. Then, a week later, after another downpour, my pet turtle ran away. I realized then that rainstorms brought bad luck.

My walk to school that day didn't do much to disprove my theory that disaster was looming. Gray clouds piled on top of each other and covered the sky, and I just knew misfortune was headed my way.

I didn't know *what* the misfortune would be, but I had a strong hunch *where* it would be: Victor Waldo Elementary. There might as well have been a bright neon sign blinking BAD LUCK, RIGHT HERE, COME AND GET IT as the largest of the cloud clusters settled over my school.

A couple times I misjudged the depth of a puddle while walking and rainwater poured into my shoes. By the time I arrived at the back gate of Victor Waldo Elementary, I was the not-so-proud owner of frizzy hair (a standard look for me on warm, humid days), wet socks, and muddy shoes. As I squished into the yard, a sickening smell wafted toward me.

"Eww," I said, wrinkling my nose. "What stinks?"

"Hey Ella," said Lucille, one of my best friends, coming up from behind me. "Oh, ugh!" She pinched her nose shut and shook her head in disgust, causing her messy red ringlets to *boing* like crazy. "I hope Jolina gets here soon so we don't have to stand here too long. It stinks." She sounded like a cross between a moose and a duck.

"I talked to Jolina last night, and she said she'd meet us on the playground. She had to get here early. There was a safety patrol meeting this morning."

"Good," said Lucille. "Then we don't have to wait around and smell whatever reeks."

As we crossed the muddy field, I scanned the playground for Jolina. I needed to ask her a question about our math homework. Most of it had completely freaked me out, so if our teacher, Ms. Carpenter, gave us a pop quiz, I'd fail for sure. Jolina Washington was my other best friend even though we were as opposite as night and day. When it came to math, Jolina was a whiz kid, and I was the kid math whizzed past.

I had two major phobias in life: spiders and mathematics. I firmly believed anything with more than four legs should not exist. I also believed the world would be a better place without fractions or long division.

The more I thought about it, the more likely it seemed my unavoidable bad luck would have something to do with math. Or spiders, but my money was on math. I had experienced a spider issue already this year, so it was math's turn to make my life miserable. I was teeter-tottering between a C and a D in the subject, and my parents had informed me if I got a D, I'd have to go to tutoring classes all summer long.

I was so intent on finding Jolina, I didn't pay attention to where I was walking.

"Ella, look out!" Lucille yelled. She yanked me back so hard I lost my balance and fell to the muddy ground.

"Lucille O'Reilly!" I squealed. "What did you do that for?" I picked myself up and tried to brush off the mud. Instead, I ended up smearing it across my shorts.

"You almost stepped on that!"

She pointed at the ground. Lying on its back was a very ugly, very wet, and very dead opossum—the source of the bad smell. Its four hairy legs stuck straight up in the air, and a frozen expression grinned at me. Flies buzzed around its stiff body.

I jumped back. "Oh, gross! I can't believe I almost stepped on it!"

Lucille grabbed my arm and pulled me away.

My shrieking, however, had caught the attention of Harry, the weird guy in our class, and he trotted over. Common sense wasn't Harry's strong point; he would take any bet someone offered him. The year before, when we were in fourth grade, a fifth-grader in the cafeteria had bet Harry five dollars he couldn't eat fifty packets of ketchup and then chug three cartons of chocolate milk without throwing up. Harry made it through the ketchup and two and half cartons of milk, then started choking. He coughed so hard the rest of the milk came out his nose (which he had said *technically* wasn't throwing up).

As Harry stared at the dead opossum, his eyes widened. "Ms. Carpenter! Ms. Carpenter! Look, a possum!" he bellowed. "It's dead. At least I think it's dead—maybe it's just playin' dead—they can do that, ya know. Do you think it's dead?"

Ms. Carpenter and several students slogged through the mud toward us.

"Sacre bleu! Ah will give you a dollar to touch zee possum, 'arry!" Jean-Pierre said. Jean-Pierre had moved from France the previous month and obviously someone had already told him about Harry's willingness to take bets.

"You're on. But you didn't say I had to use my hand, so I'll poke it with this stick." Harry pushed his glasses high up on his nose, picked up a stick lying in the grass, and reached toward the opossum.

Ms. Carpenter snatched the stick from Harry's hand.

I glanced at Harry. I'd never seen a more disappointed look. There he was, surrounded by his fellow fifth-graders and publicly stripped not only of his right to earn a dollar, but also to poke a possibly dead animal.

Ms. Carpenter's face, on the other hand, had turned a sickly green color. She covered her nose with her hand. "I'll notify the custodian about the animal. I'm sure he'll know what to do. Meanwhile, everybody go play on the far side of the field closer to the playground and stay out of this area!" She shooed us away while reaching for her walkie-talkie.

The boys let out groans of disappointment as we walked toward the playground for the precious few minutes of playtime left before the first bell.

Ms. Carpenter called after me, "Oh, Ella, do you want to call your mom and ask her to bring you some clean clothes?"

"No thanks. I'm fine." I stared down at my dirt-smeared shorts. Just my luck. I cringed at the thought of wearing the muddy clothes all day. Truthfully, I did want to call my mom, but knew I needed to find Jolina and get math help in case we had a quiz.

Clean clothes would have to wait.

CHAPTER TWO
RIGOR MORTIS

rig·or mor·tis

noun \rig-ŏr - **mor**-tis\

—temporary rigidity of muscles occurring after death

We found Jolina near the monkey bars. She was easy to spot because she wore her safety patrol belt. Weeks ago, she told me she hated wearing the belt because it was scratchy. I guess she had to wear it because of the meeting this morning. I always thought she looked pretty with it on—the bright lime green against her dark skin.

"Hey there, Jolina!" said Lucille. "You missed all the excitement!"

"Yeah, real exciting, Lucille," I muttered. "You're not the one who nearly stepped on that *thing*."

"What are you two talking about?" Jolina asked. "Did you step in dog poo again, Ella?"

I suppose it could've been worse. The week before, I'd almost twisted my ankle sliding through a pile of dog logs. I was still scraping the nastiness from the treads of my favorite boots.

Jolina didn't give me a chance to explain, though.

"After our safety patrol meeting, my stomach felt queasy, so I went to the nurse's office. She gave me a peppermint. I just now made it out to the playground." She wiggled her shoulders around, scowled, and readjusted her belt.

I looked over at Lucille, begging her with my expression not to tell Jolina about the opossum— she'd puke all over the place. Lucille must have got the message.

"Bummer. I sure hope you feel better. You don't want to miss out on Ms. Carpenter's big announcement today. Remember she said she had special news for us?" said Lucille.

I'd completely forgotten about Ms. Carpenter's surprise announcement! I was so anxious about the math homework and focused on getting Jolina's help (not to mention shaken by the little episode with the opossum), it had totally skipped my mind.

"What do you think it is?" Jolina asked.

"I don't know, but I can't wait to find out!" Lucille said.

I was just about to ask Jolina for homework help when the bell rang. Not cool. I quickly pulled her aside as we hurried to class. "I don't get it."

"Don't get what?"

"Last night's math. And I have a feeling Ms. Carpenter's going to give us a pop quiz or something. She's been pop-quiz happy lately."

I've always been a bit of a control freak. I don't like surprises—like pop quizzes. Surprises make me feel out of control. Mom thinks my control "issues" are because I'm an only child. She's a mental health counselor and knows a lot about stuff like that. But, I don't have issues; I have rules.

Like M&M's can only be eaten in pairs and must be in specific color combinations. The pencils in my pencil cup have to be sharpened after I finish my homework so they're pointy the next time I need them. Even the clothes in my closet are organized by color and season.

"Don't worry. I doubt she'll give a quiz," Jolina said.

"C'mon. You saw the rain clouds."

"Yes, and I think your whole theory about storms makes you nutso."

"Fine, I'm nutso."

Jolina smiled and rolled her eyes. "Just remember to take the quotient and—"

"Wait, what's a quotient?" I interjected.

But Jolina never got to tell me.

"Good Tuesday morning, everybody," Ms. Carpenter said as we entered the room. "Take a seat and listen up." She had regained her composure and apparently had decided our experience with the smelly stiff was in fact a teaching moment in disguise. "I know many of you saw the dead animal in the playing field this morning and have been talking about it. First of all, that was

an *opossum*, not a possum. The opossum lives in
North America, and the possum lives in Australia
and New Zealand—similar animals, but still
different. However, you will commonly hear either
animal referred to as a possum, dropping the 'o.'
Though not technically accurate, most people will
know what animal you're talking about based on
where you live.

"Secondly, I'm sure you noticed how stiff
and rigid it was. This is due to what's called *ri-gor
mor-tis.*" She pronounced the words slowly,
emphasizing each syllable, as she wrote them on
the board. "When something dies, after a period
of time the muscles stiffen, and they will stay in
whatever position they're in for several hours,
depending on the size of the animal or person."

While *I'm* fascinated by science, I wasn't so
sure how Jolina and her upset stomach were han-
dling this moment. I stole a look at her. She held
one hand over her stomach and was frantically
waving the other in the air. "Please, Ms. Carpenter,
may I get some water?"

"Yes, Jolina, but be quick. You don't want to
miss our mini-science lesson."

I was pretty sure the mini-science lesson was exactly what Jolina wanted to miss. She bolted for the door.

"So, the possum was on its back with its feet in the air when it died?" Lucille asked.

"It appears so. And because of rigor mortis," Ms. Carpenter said, pointing to the words again, "it was still in that position this morning. Like I said, it takes several hours for the muscles to loosen up again."

"Hey, I have a question," Jimmy said. "When my snake dies, if I straighten him out as rigor mortis sets in, could I throw him like a javelin?"

Jean-Pierre chimed in, "Oh yes, zat would be very cool. I would love to see zat!" He slapped Jimmy a high-five. He was learning our culture just fine.

Ms. Carpenter closed her eyes, took a deep breath, and sighed. I noticed that happened a lot when Jimmy asked questions. Our teaching moment had come to an abrupt halt.

"Everyone please take out a pencil and clear your desks," she said. "It's time for a pop quiz on last night's homework."

I knew it! Bad luck and math *had* combined forces to destroy my life. If these pop quizzes kept showing up, I'd be sunk.

I sat at my desk staring with dread at the five math problems just below the words RIGOR MORTIS. Death and math problems . . . they definitely went together. I knew it was my imagination, but the problems seemed to be sneering and throwing insults my direction. *You can't do this . . . You're not smart enough . . . You'll make a mistake and screw up . . .*

CHAPTER THREE
FAIR

fair
adverb \fer\

—in a manner that is honest or impartial
or that conforms to rules
noun \fer\
—festival; an exhibition, often accompanied
by entertainment and amusements

Given my love for order, you'd think I would have appreciated math; after all, math is very orderly. But the subject completely freaked me out. I didn't like it one bit. I didn't like it because I wasn't *good* at it, but I wasn't *good* at it because I didn't like it. It was a nasty cycle. My parents said if I could just learn to like math, I'd probably get better at it.

To be honest, that was the craziest thing I'd ever heard. Well, maybe not the craziest, but it was close. The craziest would be the time I told my mother I didn't like going out to the toolshed at night because I was afraid of spiders. She suggested I start calling all the spiders I see "Jonathan" because then they would seem more like friends and I wouldn't be scared of them.

Seriously?

The only thing that came from that brilliant idea was a bunch of squished spiders on the shed floor and a strong dislike of the name Jonathan. At any rate, I really struggled with math and would've liked nothing better than to never do it again . . . ever.

Ms. Carpenter told us she would wait to make her special announcement before P.E., the last class of the day. So at lunch, Jolina, Lucille, and I tried to guess what she was going to tell us.

"I bet she's gonna tell us she's getting married. Maybe she wants all the girls to be in her wedding! We'll probably be bridesmaids or flower girls!" Lucille whispered, clapping her hands.

Jolina shook her head. "I don't think that's it. I bet she's taking us on a really cool field trip. Like to Washington, DC, or the Mall of America."

I still felt miserable about the pop quiz and took out my frustration on my Jell-O. I jabbed my spoon repeatedly in the lemon-yellow blob until it resembled scrambled eggs. "The Mall of America is all the way in Minnesota and everyone knows Washington, DC, is a middle school field trip. I seriously doubt either of those are it," I grumbled. "It's probably just another pizza party."

Lucille knocked her shoulder against mine. "Cheer up, Ella. There're just a few weeks of school left and then we're home free! Swimming, sleepovers, and water-skiing at my uncle's lake house."

"If I'm not stuck with a tutor all summer," I reminded her.

"I bet things will end up better than you think," she replied.

"And I agree with Lucille," said Jolina. "Give yourself more credit. You're smart. You just lose it sometimes with math."

"That's the understatement of the century," I said.

A sense of dread—the feeling I'd be stuck with a tutor all summer—stayed with me through silent reading and a science lesson (not about rigor mortis).

Finally it was time to get ready for P.E. Lucille shoved her book into her desk and grabbed her homework folder. As she crammed it into her backpack, she looked at me and smiled. The moment had come to hear Ms. Carpenter's news, but I wasn't going to shove anything anywhere. I was particular about how my desk looked—everything had its special place. I carefully placed my books and pencils in their correct spots and tucked my homework folder in my backpack.

"Class, I have something very exciting to share with you," said Ms. Carpenter. She stood in front of us, hiding something behind her back, and smiled.

This was it—the big announcement. I stole a peek at Lucille and Jolina. Lucille looked like she was imagining herself in a bridesmaid dress, and

Jolina appeared to be mentally spending all her allowance at the Mall of America. As for me, I could already taste the pepperoni pizza.

"As I'm sure you're all aware, there are only three weeks left of school before summer vacation. That's not enough time to teach a whole new math unit. Therefore, the fifth-grade teachers have decided there will be no more math tests for the rest of the year."

"Sweet!" Jimmy yelled out.

"Zut alors!" said Jean-Pierre.

Was I hearing this correctly? No more math tests? Maybe my luck had finally changed. This was my dream come true and far better than any pizza party, field trip, or wedding. Life could not have gotten any better.

Cheering filled the room, and things didn't quiet down until Ms. Carpenter clapped her hands together.

"Hold on. Let me finish, please. That doesn't mean there won't be any more math."

Groans replaced the cheers.

"Instead," she paused and grinned, "we will hold Victor Waldo Elementary's first ever math fair!"

Dead silence filled the air (unless you counted the cricket chirping in the back of the room).

Surely she was joking. A math fair? Of course, I was thrilled there'd be no more tests, but a math fair didn't exactly seem . . . well, fair. However, when given the choice, I'd take a math fair over a test any day. While the situation wasn't ideal, it certainly wasn't horrible.

"What exactly is a math fair?" asked Lucille, a note of disappointment in her voice. So much for her hopes of being a bridesmaid.

"It's a chance for us to look back on the math we've covered this year. You can work together in teams to design a display booth with posters and props about a math unit you've chosen. Then, on the day of the fair, everyone will walk around and visit the other classrooms and view their displays. It'll be a fun way to review everything, and I'm sure you would agree it beats taking more tests."

While I did agree it beat doing a bunch of tests, it was crystal clear to me her definition of *fun* was way different than mine. Still, it sounded pretty painless.

"Can we pick our own teams?" someone asked.

"Yes, you may. You'll need three or four people per team," Ms. Carpenter replied.

"What about our math unit? Can we pick that, too?"

"Sort of," she said. "I've written down the units we've covered this year and put them in this hat." She brought out a ball cap from behind her back. "Each team will draw from the hat to see what topic they'll review. I'll give you a few minutes to put your teams together, then I'll walk around with the hat."

I immediately looked toward Jolina and Lucille, and we scooted our desks together, waiting our turn to draw. I watched as topics like equivalent fractions, long division, and multiplication were pulled out of the hat. Ms. Carpenter came around to our desks, and I looked anxiously at Lucille and Jolina.

"I don't want to pick. One of you do it," I said.

"Oh, I'll pick it!" said Jolina. I could tell by the squeal in her voice she considered this more fun than her imagined field trip. She dropped her hand into the hat and plucked out a small folded piece of paper.

Opening it, she read aloud, "Time conversions."

I took back what I had thought earlier. The math fair had just gotten painfully horrible. A tight knot formed in my stomach. Anything but time conversions! I was always forgetting how to do them. Could life possibly get any worse?

"Oh!" Ms. Carpenter exclaimed, interrupting my downward-spiraling depression. "I almost forgot. Two more things. Number one, there will be guest judges who will award first-, second-, and third-prize ribbons for each class. They'll also pick *one* Best of Show project out of all the classes. That group will receive a special prize. I'll let you know who the judges are and what the prize is as we get closer to the day of the fair. I won't be a judge, but I *will* be grading your projects—which brings me to my second item. Since this is a major project we will be working on for a couple of weeks both in and out of class, your math fair presentation will count as two test grades, so make sure your team does its best work."

Two test grades! I closed my eyes and dropped my head into my hands. The math fair was not an improvement at all; it was a complete disaster. If the math fair didn't go well for me, neither would my summer break. I turned to stare out the window. The gray storm clouds hung heavy with rain and a faint rumble of thunder sounded in the distance. Another storm? As it was, the score stood rainstorms 4, me 0.

CHAPTER FOUR
DEAD BALL

dead ball

noun **ded** bawl\\

—a phenomenon in many sports in which the
ball is deemed temporarily not playable

Ms. Carpenter's announcement that our
math fair grade would equal two test
grades made my head hurt. I almost
didn't hear her tell us to stack our chairs and get
ready to go to P.E.

P.E. was the one bright spot in my day. I looked
forward to it for a couple reasons. First of all, it

meant my school day was almost over and I could go home. Second, despite the fact that I wasn't athletically gifted, I still enjoyed the relay races, fitness tests, soccer games, and even badminton. My favorite game by far was kickball—especially when our class was playing Mrs. Fyffe's, like we were today. Coach Harris flipped a coin to see who would kick first; we won.

Jolina, Lucille, and I sat next to each other on the bench, waiting for our chance to kick. My friends' non-stop chatter about the math fair annoyed me, and I tried my best to tune them out as they planned ways to decorate our display. Instead, I focused my attention on the game, determined to enjoy it. The rain was holding off, and soon our class scored two runs.

When it was Jimmy's turn to kick, he did his "crazy leg" dance and bellowed, "Watch out, far field! Here comes the crazy leg!"

Everyone in Ms. Carpenter's class cheered because we all knew Jimmy's crazy leg kick was the most spectacular thing that could happen for our team. Kindergarteners through fifth graders knew all about Jimmy's skills with a kickball. His funky little dance always culminated in a kick so hard and fierce it was uncatchable.

Always.

Until today.

Jimmy let loose with a tremendous kick and the ball ripped through the air, soaring into far left field. He sprinted around first and second as several kids from Mrs. Fyffe's class scrambled to chase after the ball. However, they skidded to a stop when they reached it. We watched, waiting for them to pick up the ball and throw it home, but no one moved. They just stood still, gawking at the ground.

"Pick up the ball and throw it!" Coach Harris hollered.

One of them yelled something back to Coach Harris, but I couldn't understand what was said. He rolled his eyes, tossed down his clipboard, and jogged toward left field. Jimmy rounded home plate and launched into his victory dance, but no one paid him any attention. We were all watching the group in the field. Curiosity got the better of us and we scurried over to see what the big stink was.

And big stink was putting it lightly.

Apparently Mr. Leeford, the custodian, hadn't had a chance to remove the dead opossum; it was still lying there on its back with its legs sticking straight up in the air and the flies were still buzzing around. Only now, a kickball was wedged between its front and back legs. Nobody *alive* had ever managed to catch one of Jimmy's crazy leg balls, so in an odd way it seemed appropriate it was caught, so to speak, by something *dead*.

The sight of the dead opossum holding a ball was all the boys needed to whoop and cheer. It was also all poor Jolina needed to throw up. Harry and Jean-Pierre, shouting that they finally had confirmation that the opossum was in fact dead and not just faking it, jumped up in the air and chest-bumped each other.

Jimmy pointed to the animal. "Dude! That's crazy! It's the most awesome thing ever!" He turned to us to slap high-fives but suddenly stopped and asked Coach Harris, "Hey Coach, am I out? This doesn't count as a catch, does it, Coach?"

Coach Harris, clearly distracted by a dead animal and thirty-two kids who were either cheering, screaming, or vomiting, glared at Jimmy and growled, "Be useful, Jimmy. Take Jolina to the nurse and then go find Mr. Leeford. Ask him to come here as quickly as possible and to bring a shovel!"

He ran his hand over his face and appeared, for the first time, to really take in the chaos that surrounded him. He fumbled around, grabbed his whistle, and blew it. "Enough!" he yelled. "Everyone go back to the gym and get ready for dismissal!"

I found it ironic that something dead had added so much life to my day. I hadn't the faintest idea how Coach Harris would retrieve the kickball or what he would do about the opossum, or even if Jimmy was out or not, but it had made for a very interesting time in P.E., and, for a brief moment, I had forgotten about my math problem.

CHAPTER FIVE
CONTROL FREAK

con·trol freak

noun \kŏn-**trohl** freek\

—person with a strong need to exercise control

I barely made it through the front door before the rain started pouring. I could hear Mom on the phone in the kitchen as I headed in to grab a snack. I plopped down on the bar stool, exhaled a deep sigh, and began to peel an orange.

"I completely agree with you . . . Mmm . . . hmmm . . . Well, I need to go. Ella's home now so I'm going to see how her day went. She's sighing deeply while peeling fruit . . . Yes, never a good sign."

After putting down the phone, she came and sat on the stool next to me.

"Rough day at school, huh?"

"Quite possibly the worst in history," I replied. "Unless, of course, you count the time when Jimmy brought his pet spider—pardon me, pet Jonathan—to school. Which, in fact, was a Chilean rose tarantula, and which, after escaping, decided to make its new home in my desk."

She smiled. "Yes, well, that would be hard to top. Why don't you tell me what happened that made *today* so awful?"

I told her all about my wet shoes, frizzy hair, muddy clothes, the close encounter with the dead opossum, the pop quiz, and the dreaded math fair. I had her complete sympathy until I got to the part when the opossum caught the kickball. She laughed until tears ran down her face.

"Sounds like that poor possum had a far worse day than you did," she said, wiping her eyes.

"Yeah, but at least his math worries, if he even had any, are over. What am I going to do about this math fair? Ms. Carpenter says it counts for two math tests. Two, Mom!" I ripped away a small chunk of peel from the orange. "You know how freaked out I get about math. Luckily Lucille and Jolina are both on my team. Hopefully they'll get us a good grade."

"You have to carry your own weight on this, too, Ella. You can't just let your friends do all the work and sponge off their effort."

"I know," I grumped. "But for some reason they're all happy about doing math."

She smiled. "Lucille doesn't ever seem to get upset over anything. That's why I call her Happy-Go-Lucky-Lucy."

I called her Lucy-Goosey, for the same reason. Lucille was so relaxed about life that her little brother could dump cat food in her drawers of clean clothes and she would laugh about it.

Mom continued. "As for Jolina, she has too much common sense to let something like a math fair get her worked up."

"Yeah—that and the fact she's brilliant at everything," I muttered.

She sighed. "What would it take to make *you* happy about doing math?"

"It would make me happy to never deal with it again. My stomach gets queasy, my palms get sweaty. I forget steps. I'm always second-guessing my work. I'm probably the only person in my class who doesn't get it. Actually, I think I'm allergic to math and should probably just stop doing it."

"You're not allergic, Ella. And you can't stick your head in the sand and hope math goes away."

I sat up straighter. "It works for ostriches."

"You're not an ostrich, young lady. And I promise you that you aren't the only kid who 'doesn't get it.' Everybody has trouble sometimes. The key is not to let a few mistakes affect your attitude about something for the rest of your life."

"You're doing it again, Mom—treating me like one of your clients."

She squeezed my hand and ignored my remark. "The most important thing is to work through your fear of making a mistake. You need to process those feelings."

Processing feelings was a big deal to her. I actually didn't know what she meant half the time, but I always smiled and acted like I understood.

She kissed the top of my head. "You love science, right?"

I nodded.

"Science and math are closely related. Scientists look at a situation, explore and experiment with it, and figure out the best way to go about solving their problem. They take it slow. Step by step. Just imagine when you're working on a math question you're, in a sense, really doing a science experiment. See what happens, okay?"

I got up and tossed the orange peel bits in the trash. The shredded pieces looked a lot like my summer plans.

She continued talking. "Look at all the scientific discoveries made from mistakes. Louis Pasteur accidentally found a vaccine for rabies. Alexander Fleming discovered penicillin. Even Silly Putty came about all because of a mistake."

I raised my eyebrows. "Come on, really? Silly Putty?"

She smiled, reached for her apron, and tied it around her waist. "Now, I've got a surprise for you. Guess who I was talking to on the phone?"

I shrugged. "Ms. Carpenter?"

"Nope. Guess again."

"Dad?"

She made a buzzer sound. "Ehh. Wrong answer. I was talking to your Aunt Willa!"

"Wacky Willa!"

"Yes. She's back in the country for a few months—until September." She paused and smiled at me. "Actually, she's having some renovations done on her condo and she's going to stay with us for about a month!"

"Really? That's awesome!"

My Aunt Willa was a photojournalist who spent a ton of time traveling around the world to pretty cool places. Because of some of the things she'd done just to take photos—like hang off the side of a mountain, swim with sharks, and crazy stuff like that—she'd nicknamed herself Wacky Willa.

She was also my favorite aunt. We both loved mysteries and the color turquoise and we agreed that pizza with pepperoni and pineapple was, without a doubt, the best in the world. Plus, she knew I collected turtles, so each time she went somewhere, she'd send me a new one for my collection. I had close to thirty turtles from all over the world.

"So, when does she get here?"

"Tomorrow." Mom shifted her feet and thought for a moment, then spoke. "Here's the thing though, Ella. Since we've turned the guest room into my home office, she's going to need to stay with you in your room."

"Oh."

My room was . . . well, *my* room. It's not that I didn't want to share; it was that I was very particular about how my room looked. A vein in my forehead began to throb. My room was like my desk at school—everything had its own special place. My furniture was evenly spaced along the walls and my books were alphabetized by title. My turtle collection was meticulously arranged on my dresser, based on which continent and then country the turtles came from. I liked my room a certain way and didn't want someone coming in and changing things—even my favorite aunt.

"What about the sofa? It's pretty comfortable and compared to camping I bet she'd love it."

"Don't be silly. She's not going to sleep on our sofa for a month. Besides, she'll need a place to store her things. I don't want her feeling like she has to live out of a suitcase."

"Maybe we could convert the garage into a bedroom? I know there's no air conditioning, but she could sleep with the garage door open."

"Ella." Mom's tone warned me her mind was made up, and once she was set on something, there was no convincing her otherwise.

I tossed my hands up in surrender. "Fine."

"Thank you for being so understanding," she said (although, in my personal opinion, I thought it came out a bit sarcastic). "She's also bringing Chewy with her. As long as he spends most of his time outdoors, your dad is okay with him being here."

Chewy was a bulldozer disguised as a dog and he had the IQ of a walnut. Aunt Willa had found him as a stray puppy eating from her garbage can. He stayed with her friends when she traveled. We'd never had him at our house before because our backyard didn't have a fence. But Dad had built one during his last vacation, which made us ready to Chewy-sit.

Mom opened the refrigerator door. "Now help me figure out what we should have for dinner. Oh! I know—how about some meatloaf?"

I dropped my head in my hands and sighed.

As I got ready for bed that night, I looked around my room. My bedspread was wrinkle-free, and my desk completely clear, except for my bright turquoise pencil cup. I'd dusted each of my turtles after dinner and made space on my dresser for the new one I knew Aunt Willa would bring. While I hoped she wouldn't mess things up too much, the throbbing vein in my forehead said I didn't really believe I would get off that easy. I told myself to relax and thought of all the fun things Aunt Willa and I would do: hours of girl talk, pedicure parties, maybe even a photography lesson or two. Plus, she was an adult, so I was sure she'd keep the room tidy. What could go wrong?

CHAPTER SIX
ABOUT-FACE

a·bout-face

noun \ă-**bowt**-fays\

—a reversal of attitude, behavior, or point of view

I met up with Jolina and Lucille at the back gate the next morning. They were deep in conversation about a new kid joining our class.

"How do you know he'll be in our class?" Jolina asked.

"They're our new neighbors who moved in yesterday," Lucille explained. "I got a chance to meet the whole family. He told me his parents just enrolled him, and his teacher is going to be Ms. Carpenter."

"Who moves and enrolls their kid in a new school when there's only three weeks left in the year?" I asked as we started walking across the field. I scanned the ground, but thankfully there were no dead animals to be seen.

"His parents are in the military and transferred here from somewhere in Texas."

"Oh, so he's an army brat," said Jolina.

"Jolina! That's not nice," Lucille sputtered, brushing her messy red curls back from her face. "Why would you call him a brat? You haven't even met him."

"No, you goof. I don't mean he's an actual brat. That's just an expression. It means military kids have a sort of spunkiness and knack for adjusting to new places."

I laughed at her. "You always sound like a dictionary."

"My grandpa was in the military." She held out her arm with the charm bracelet she always wore. There were so many things attached to it, I wasn't sure what all was there. "See the anchor charm? That represents the Navy. He was a submariner during World War II—before he married my grandma."

"So, what's the brat's name?" I asked Lucille.

"Umm," Jolina interrupted. "That's not quite the right way to use the word—*that* really is insulting."

"His name is Jonathan," Lucille said.

I shuddered and my foot involuntarily stomped the ground. Jolina gave me a funny look, but I chose to ignore it.

"Just wait 'til you see him, Ella. He's cute and has this great Southern drawl," Lucille said.

I looked at Jolina; we both rolled our eyes. Lucille had more crushes than she did freckles.

"At the moment, I don't care if he's cute or not. I have bigger issues—like the math fair. Although," I mimicked my mom's voice, "I am going to 'make a conscious effort to have a better attitude.'" I made bunny-ear quotes with my fingers.

Jolina knocked her shoulder against mine. "Well, just between us, you aren't off to a great start," she said.

I laughed. "Yeah, I guess not. I've got time to improve though. But hey, guess what?"

ABOUT-FACE   41

"What?"

"Mom told me my Aunt Willa is going to stay with us for a whole month while her place gets renovated." I adjusted my backpack on my shoulders. "The only bummer is *I* have to share my room with her. I just hope she doesn't move things around."

Jolina turned to me. "Ella, you're really particular about your room. Are you going to be able to handle this?"

"It'll be fine. After all, she's an adult—how much damage can Wacky Willa do?"

Lucille's mouth dropped open. "You call her Wacky Willa to her face?"

"Sometimes." I laughed at her shocked expression. "It's okay—she gave herself the nickname."

"She's a photographer, right?" said Lucille.

"Photojournalist," I corrected.

"What's the difference?"

"I don't know. I'll have to ask her. I just know she's pretty insistent she's not *just* a photographer." I kicked a rock out of my way. "I wish I could be like her. Go to new places. See unusual things. Eat bizarre foods. *Not* do any dumb math!"

As we neared the playground, Lucille nudged me in the ribs. "Look over by the picnic tables. See the boy with blond hair wearing the green T-shirt? That's Jonathan. I'll introduce you."

We walked over to where Jonathan perched on top of a table. He looked a little lonely as he gazed at the student-filled playground, but perked up when he saw Lucille approaching. She raised her arm and waved. He smiled and waved back.

"Hey Jonathan! I want to introduce you to my two best friends. They're also in Ms. Carpenter's class."

"Nice to meet y'all," he replied, climbing down from the table. He was slightly taller than I was, with a wiry build and dark brown eyes.

"Lucille tells us you just moved here from Texas," I said. "That's where my grandparents live. What part are you from?"

"Fort Sam Houston—it's near San Antonio. My dad's a doctor, and the fort is a medical training base."

The four of us chatted until the bell rang and then we escorted Jonathan to the classroom. Ms. Carpenter found a seat for him near Lucille.

When it was time for morning math, we divided into our groups to work on the math fair; Ms. Carpenter brought Jonathan over to us.

"Since there are only three people in your group and you have already established a rapport with Jonathan, I'm going to put him in your group," she said.

Lucille waited until Ms. Carpenter walked away. "What does she mean we've 'established a report'?"

"Not report. Rapport—the *t* is silent," Jolina said. "It means we have a friendly relationship and we'll probably all work well together."

I was happy because more people in the group meant more brain cells working on our project. That increased my odds of getting a good grade. Plus, Jonathan's dad was a doctor, which meant he must be mega smart. Maybe Jonathan was mega smart, too. The school day had just started, and it was already better than the day before.

CHAPTER SEVEN

PHOTOJOURNALISM

pho·to·jour·nal·ism
noun \foh-toh-**jur**-nă-liz-ĕm\

—journalism in which written copy is subordinate
to photographic presentation of news stories

I rushed home after school, hoping Aunt Willa
had already arrived. I threw open the front
door. "Aunt Willa? Are you here?"

"She *was*, but she went back to her condo to
get more stuff!" Mom yelled. "Come to your room.
I need help moving your dresser."

"Moving my dresser?" I tossed my backpack toward the dining room table and sprinted down the hall to my room.

I skidded to a halt and gripped my doorframe in horror as I stared into my room. It looked as though it had been trashed by a posse of two-year-olds. Three beat-up suitcases were piled haphazardly on my bed. The rumpled blankets reminded me of my wadded up sheets of math homework. On my desk sat a heavy-duty black camera bag. My cup of sharpened pencils had been knocked over and pencils lay scattered across the desktop and on the floor. Aunt Willa's signature safari hat hung on the back of the chair. My bathroom door, which was next to the bed, was barricaded with a camera tripod and a crooked stack of plastic tubs. My desk, which normally was against the wall, was shoved into the corner and the dresser stood in the middle of the room. Mom rested against it, panting slightly. "I've made room in your closet for your dresser. We need to put it there so we can bring down the extra mattress to put on the floor."

"What extra mattress?"

Mom pointed up. "There's an old twin mattress in the attic. Dad will bring it down when he gets home."

I grimaced.

"Don't worry. It's been wrapped in plastic—no spiders. Give me a hand with your dresser. It's too heavy to lift by myself, and it isn't sliding very well on the carpet." A strand of hair had come loose from her ponytail, and she brushed it away from her face.

I went to the other side of my dresser, and we weeble-wobbled it into the closet.

"Whew!" Mom plopped on my bed and caught the top suitcase as it slid onto her lap. "What a workout."

I sat next to her and looked around. "Hmm . . . wow. She sure brought a lot of stuff. You said she went back to get *more*?"

Mom laughed at my concerned expression. "She didn't want to leave all her expensive camera equipment at her condo—not with all the dust and dirt that would be made during the renovation."

I looked at my dresser stuffed in the closet. "Where did you put my turtle collection that was on the dresser?"

"I've boxed it up for now and put it on the shelf in your closet. I'm afraid it's in the far back and barricaded by some of Aunt Willa's things. She brought you a new turtle, but it's in the box with the others."

"Oh." I felt the vein in my forehead start to throb again. I had been looking forward to seeing what the new turtle looked like, and now I'd have to wait at least a month until my room was back to normal.

My things were being moved.

Already.

Without my permission.

Even though the only furniture left was my bed and desk, my room looked trashed with all of Aunt Willa's stuff. I knew with another mattress it would feel cramped and maybe even uncomfortable. I guess I hadn't really thought about how having a roommate would work.

Of course, I had *my* bed and, naturally, Aunt Willa would need a place to sleep. The spare mattress in the attic seemed like a good option. No doubt Aunt Willa had slept in worse conditions when she traveled. A mattress on the floor would probably feel like sleeping on clouds to her.

The front door slammed.

"Yoo-hoo!"

I jumped up from the bed. "Aunt Willa!" I yelled.

"Ella Bella!" she yelled back.

We collided in the hallway. She wrapped her arms around me and squeezed tight. I gave her a mongo bear hug. She wore what she called her "uniform"—khaki cargo pants and short-sleeve shirt. Her hair was pulled back in a braid in an attempt to control it, but frizzled bits poked out all over, making her look like she stuck her finger in an electric socket. I kept my arm around her as we walked back to my room.

"So," Aunt Willa said, "I hear we're going to be roomies."

"Yeppers," I said. "You don't snore, do you?"

"Nope. Chewy's the only one who snores," she teased. At least, I *hoped* she was teasing.

"Where is Chewy anyway?"

"He's out back, chasing squirrels. I'll bring him in at night, but he'll spend his days outside."

Mom pushed herself off my bed and shuffled toward the door. "I'm going to check on dinner. We'll eat in about an hour."

Aunt Willa took a step back. "Let me take a look at you." She reached out and gently touched my hair. "Your hair is darker now—and it's past your shoulders." She slid next to me and measured her shoulder against mine. "Ah-ha! Just as I thought—you grew. You're much taller than I remember."

"And you're tanner than I remember," I said.

She lightly smacked the top of my head. "I was on assignment in Africa."

"Whoa, cool! Where in Africa?"

"All over," she said, walking to the desk.

"What were you taking pictures of?" I asked.

"Just wildlife this time." She opened her camera bag. "Elephants, rhinos, that sort of thing."

I sat down on my bed and shifted her luggage off to the side. "That reminds me, I promised my friend Lucille I'd ask you what the difference is between a photographer and a photojournalist."

"That's easy." Aunt Willa stopped rummaging through the camera bag and reached for a leather-bound folder. "This is my portfolio. It's where I keep the photographs I've taken so I can show them to others. In a nutshell, as a photojournalist, I try to educate or tell a story with my pictures." She pulled one out and handed it to me. Mounds of garbage, many of them bigger than my house, filled the black-and-white photograph. Birds circled overhead and in the distance a bulldozer pushed more trash. What caught my eye the most was a boy who looked to be about my age with three or four dark specks on his face—I'm pretty sure they were flies. He stood next to the trash heap closest to the edge of the photo. All he was wearing was a pair of torn shorts. He didn't even have shoes. His grimy hands clutched a torn rag full of half-rotted food. He looked into the camera with an empty stare. I could practically smell the stench from the landfill and feel the emptiness in the boy's stomach.

Aunt Willa shook her head. "Poverty is never a nice story, but it's still one that needs to be told," she said. She took the photograph from my hands and then pulled out a pizza flyer. Pepperoni was front and center. "This is an example of what a commercial photographer does. They use their photographs for advertising and publicity. And there's also personal photography like for weddings and such. One isn't better than the other;

they're just different. And I am proud of the stories I tell with my camera."

"I think I can remember that," I said quietly. The image of the hungry boy lingered in my memory.

Mom popped her head through the door. "Dad just pulled into the driveway. I've asked him to bring down your mattress."

Aunt Willa spun around and smiled at me. "Your bed is almost here!"

"Wait. *My* bed?"

Mom nodded. "Yes, dear. We thought we'd let Willa take the real bed since she's been roughing it in Africa for the last couple months."

Aunt Willa shot me a sideways look. "You don't mind, do you?"

"No . . . No, of course not," I stuttered . . . and lied. This time I could feel the vein in my forehead pop out.

"You're a sweet girl," Aunt Willa said. She kissed me on the cheek. "I'll come and help with dinner." She and Mom headed down the hall to the kitchen.

"I'm going to change out of my school clothes," I called after them, shutting the door and resting against it. I closed my eyes and counted to ten. It was a trick Mom taught me to do when I felt upset. It gave me time to think before reacting— or at least that's what it was supposed to do. I opened my eyes, looked around the room, and decided I should probably count again, maybe even to twenty.

I turned toward my dresser, remembered it was in the closet, and opened my top drawer for a clean shirt.

My top drawer was empty.

My second drawer was empty, too! I slammed it shut.

I pulled on the third drawer. It didn't budge. I jerked harder and smacked my funny bone on the closet door. The drawer opened an inch. I gave one hard tug and the drawer spewed out socks, underwear, and T-shirts—things that were *supposed* to be folded and in the top two drawers. I investigated the last drawer. It was also overstuffed with clothes. Apparently, Mom forgot to tell me she'd made room for Aunt Willa's things in my dresser. I hadn't planned on that. Of course, I hadn't really planned on giving up my bed, either.

It wasn't that I minded giving up my bed for Aunt Willa; I just wish Mom had asked me first. I closed my eyes and counted to one hundred.

CHAPTER EIGHT

CHEW

chew

verb \choo\

—to crush, grind, or gnaw (as food) with
or as with the teeth
—to injure, destroy, or consume as if by chewing

After I changed clothes, I grabbed some sheets and made my bed—er, my mattress—and joined Mom, Dad, and Aunt Willa in the kitchen.

"I bet you're looking forward to some good home-style cooking for a change, right Willa?" Dad said.

"Oh yeah," Aunt Willa said. "I've sure missed American food."

"Well, you're in luck. Tonight it's barbequed chicken and potato salad."

We gathered around the table, Dad said the blessing, and we dug in. Aunt Willa told us stories of hiding in bushes for hours, sometimes days, waiting for a rhinoceros or leopard to show. And there was the time she saw hyenas and a whole bunch of crocodiles fight over a dead hippo.

I turned to Aunt Willa. "Remind me to tell you my dead possum story later. For some reason, I think you'll like it."

She raised her eyebrows. "I'm curious."

After we'd stuffed ourselves, Mom brought out a pan of dark chocolate chunk brownies and sent Dad to the kitchen to make coffee. "I just read somewhere that dark chocolate can help prevent heart disease and improve brain function. So I say these brownies are health food," Mom said.

I sure wasn't going to argue. If eating brown-ies could help me get an A on the math project,

I'd eat the whole pan. In exchange for an extra brownie, I offered to clear the table and wash the dishes.

I still hadn't finished my homework, so after cleaning up, I spread my school stuff out on the living room rug and worked as Mom, Dad, and Aunt Willa drank coffee and talked. I'd completed both my spelling and social studies work when I heard scratching at the back door.

"It sounds like Chewy wants in now," Aunt Willa said.

"I'll get him," I said, jumping up.

I'd barely opened the door when Chewy barreled through, knocking me over. He bounded into the living room, ears flopping up and down. I picked myself up, locked the door, and went back to join the others.

Chewy had sniffed out Aunt Willa's location and plopped himself down in front of her. His butt was right on top of my notebook and his wagging tail sent my pencil flying across the room.

"Chewy, get off the notebook," Aunt Willa said, pulling on his collar. He stood long enough for me to grab my stuff. I scowled at the sight of my wrinkled assignments and ran my hand over them to try to smooth out the papers.

"Sorry about that, Ella. He's all brawn and no brain."

"It's okay," I mumbled. I picked up my homework and set it on the dining room table, out of harm's way. I didn't want Chewy to think I was mad at him. I knelt down beside him and rubbed his ears. His back leg thumped up and down quickly.

"He does know *I'm* the one scratching his ears, right?" I said to Aunt Willa. His brown eyes stared at me and he cocked his head. He was cute, even if he was destructive.

"Who knows what that dog knows! I just keep him because I love him too much to get rid of him. Plus, he's a great watchdog. I feel safe with him around. If he didn't try to eat everything in sight, he'd be the perfect dog."

"Is that why you named him Chewy?"

At the mention of his name, he turned around and slurped me in the face. I pushed him away in disgust and reached for the napkin next to Mom's coffee cup to wipe dog saliva off my face.

"Yes. I have to be very careful about what I leave out. Thankfully, though, he's never eaten one of my cameras."

Dad reached over and scratched one of Chewy's ears. He glanced at his watch. "It's getting late Ella-vator. Time for you to get ready for bed."

"Dad—you know I don't like that nickname."

He grinned. "I know, but you keep growing up. Get it—*growing* up, instead of *going* up?"

I smirked. "Yeah, I get it—except elevators go down, too."

"Well, let's hope you don't start shrinking." He winked.

"Can I please stay up longer? It's Aunt Willa's first night here."

"And she'll be here for a whole month. Off to bed."

I rolled my eyes. "Fine." I gave Chewy a good-night pat on the head and stood.

"Goodnight, roomie," said Aunt Willa. "I'll try to be quiet when I come in. Chewy will be, too—I promise. He can be very stealthy when he needs to be."

I stopped. "He's sleeping in my room, *too*?"

"Yeah. When I first come back from long trips, he barks all night if he's not near me." She caressed his face between her hands. "Such a big baby. But don't worry. He'll sleep on the floor by my bed—it'll be like he's not even there."

CHAPTER NINE
ANNEX

an·nex

verb \ă-neks\

—to take possession of something

My wacky Aunt Willa was right—it *was* like Chewy the stealth dog wasn't even there on the floor . . . mainly because he wasn't *there* at all! Chewy must have decided my mattress looked far more comfortable than his assigned spot of carpet. Somewhere around two o'clock in the morning, I woke up and realized I was no longer on my mattress—I was on the floor. I felt around for my pillow but instead my fingers landed on a wet nose. Squinting through the darkness, I saw Chewy's humongous head had taken over my pillow.

Actually, Chewy had taken over my *entire* bed.

He had climbed onto the mattress and shoved me off!

Aunt Willa was right about two things: he could definitely be stealthy . . . and he snored.

I tugged on his collar. "Chewy," I whispered.

He responded with a snort. Man, he had bad breath!

I pushed with both hands.

He probably weighed as much as I did *if* I was soaking wet, wearing a parka, and holding a bowling ball in each hand. He didn't budge.

I climbed onto my mattress and laid down back-to-back with him. I braced my hands and feet against the desk and slowly straightened my arms and legs, hoping I could shove him off the other side.

No such luck.

Sighing, I stood and felt around the desk for my alarm. My fingertips found it. I snatched my pillow from under Chewy's head and grabbed my blanket from the mattress. Apparently *I* would be sleeping in the living room.

On my way out, I tripped over one of Aunt Willa's suitcases and fell against the doorknob. I was pretty sure there'd be a lovely bruise on my arm in the morning. I tossed the pillow on the sofa and curled up under my blanket.

I'd just drifted back to sleep when the alarm blared in my ears. I dragged my feet to my room and collected the school clothes I'd laid out the night before. Chewy was snoring away in my bed. I glared at him and kicked the mattress before walking into my bathroom to get ready. The mirror showed the unfortunate results of not enough sleep; dark circles surrounded my puffy eyes. Even my hair looked tired. It fell limp down my back. It was *not* the look I was going for. I quickly braided it, hoping I would somehow end up looking better than I felt.

I slumped into the kitchen and grabbed a bagel. Dad took one look at me and let me have a sip of his coffee. I kissed him good-bye (Mom was still sleeping) and walked to school. As usual, Jolina and Lucille were waiting for me at the back gate. I put my hand up to stop them before they could say anything.

"Before you ask, I didn't sleep well last night," I grumbled. "Aunt Willa's dog decided to take over my bed in the middle of the night. I had to move to the sofa."

Lucille unzipped her backpack and offered me a couple gummy bears from the emergency stash she kept for me. "Aww, Ella. I'm sorry the dog commanded your bed."

I gladly took them and gave her a smile. "Thanks."

"I'm pretty sure you mean *commandeered*, not *commanded*," said Jolina.

"Really?" Lucille shrugged. "I thought I got that word right."

"No—*commandeered* means took over. *Commanded* means gave orders."

I puffed my cheeks out. "Actually, *commanded* works just as good. Chewy ordered me off the bed with his big hairy body and yucky dog breath. And to make matters worse, when I finally did fall asleep, I had a math fair nightmare. Ms. Carpenter was dressed like a clown, pedaling a unicycle while juggling math books. And Jimmy hurled javelins shaped like snakes at possums, and Jean-Pierre handed out rulers and calculators for carnival prizes. Oh yeah, and Harry took bets on how many erasers he could fit in his nose—which oddly enough was the only realistic part of the whole dream."

"That's right!" Jolina said. "I remember last year when Harry did that. It was crazy how the paramedics used those fancy pliers to get the erasers out. How many did he get up his nose, anyway?"

I shrugged. "I can't remember."

Lucille laughed. She draped one arm over Jolina's shoulders and the other over mine as we walked to our classroom. "Ella, you're worrying about the math fair way too much. The four of us are going to put together a great display, and it will be just fine," she said.

CHAPTER TEN
POSTHUMOUS

post·hu·mous

adjective **pos**-chŭ-mŭs\\

—coming or happening after death

The incident with the opossum and the kickball spread through the school faster than last year's lice epidemic. Due to the opossum's astonishing ability to catch one of Jimmy's crazy leg balls, it achieved the popularity status of a prom queen, only with far less effort. Even Jonathan already knew about it.

All the boys respectfully referred to the opossum as Morty (short for rigor mortis). Lucille found some pictures of baby opossums online and brought them in to show us in class. They actually looked really cute, and we felt kinda bad Morty had died. We had no idea where Mr. Leeford had buried him, or even *if* he had buried him. (Harry said Morty could've gone to the Great Dumpster in the Sky.) Even so, Jimmy made a miniature tombstone for him out of Play-Doh, inscribed with MORTY, THE ONE WHO CAUGHT THE UNCATCHABLE BALL, and kept it on his desk.

Coincidently, my own level of popularity had increased overnight simply because I was the one who "discovered" Morty in the first place. Discovered, stepped on. What's the difference?

After school, Jonathan, Lucille, Jolina, and I all went to my house to work on our math fair project.

Mom brought out a stack of peanut butter and jelly sandwiches, along with glasses of lemonade, and set them down on the coffee table.

"Where's Aunt Willa?" I said.

"She's here," Mom said, "developing some photos."

"I thought you needed a dark room to do that."

"Yeah, you do. She's using your bathroom." She headed out of the room but then called back over her shoulder, "Use the hall bathroom from now on, okay?"

I sighed and rubbed my temple. "Okay."

Jolina cocked her head. "Your aunt uses film?"

"She uses both a film and digital camera, but she likes film better. She says it's 'purer,' whatever *that* means."

Chewy barked and scratched at the back door.

"Go away, Chewy!" I said.

"Chewy? Is that short for Chewbacca?" asked Jonathan.

I held up one of Aunt Willa's mangled shoes. "No."

"We might as well get started," Lucille said. She picked up a sandwich and took a bite.

I flopped onto the sofa. "This project is math *un*-fair."

"Hey, you said you were going to have a good attitude about this," Jolina reminded me.

Jonathan leaned over the back of my dad's favorite chair. "What's wrong? I think the math fair sounds like fun."

"Yeah, I'd rather do this than take a test, that's for sure," said Lucille.

"You'd rather do what than take a test?" Aunt Willa came into the room, trailing a strong smell of vinegar behind her and wearing a pair of safety goggles on top of her head.

"Hi, Aunt Willa," I said. I wrinkled my nose and sniffed the air.

"Good afternoon, sweetie," she said, joining me on the sofa. "Sorry about the chemical smell. I've been developing some photos."

"I can tell."

Lucille turned to her. "We have to do a math fair at school and it's worth two test grades. *Most* of us here think it'll be fun, but *one* person"—she pointed at me—"is being a party pooper."

Aunt Willa feigned surprised. "No!" she gasped.

I rolled my eyes, but the others laughed.

"We get to make posters and displays, and the day of the fair we'll get to walk around checking out all the entries. It beats sitting at our desks all day," said Jolina, reaching for a sandwich.

I sighed. "At least that part will be fun. I just wish we'd been assigned anything but time conversions. I'm always forgetting how to do those."

"Well," Aunt Willa said, "maybe the math fair will help with that."

"Maybe. Crazier things have happened lately," I muttered. I grabbed a glass of lemonade and took a gulp.

"I have a great idea for the display," Jonathan said. He cleared his throat. "We could put Morty on our poster."

Lemonade shot out my mouth and nose and I started coughing.

"Ewww!" said Jolina, immediately putting down her sandwich.

Aunt Willa jumped up and ran to the kitchen. She returned seconds later with a roll of paper towels. "Who's Morty?"

"He's the possum I told you about." I took the towels from her and turned to Jonathan. "Number one, we don't know where he's buried. Number two, don't you think attaching a dead animal to our poster is kind of gross? And number three, what does Morty have to do with time conversions?"

"No, no, no . . . I don't mean we actually put *him* on our poster," Jonathan said. "What I mean is, how cool would it be to list different animals from a mouse to an elephant or something big and show how long it takes for rigor mortis to wear off of each one? We could make a chart showing the hours, then do the math and convert everything to minutes, and then to seconds." He paused to catch his breath. "It would be like a memorial to Morty. I know you may think it sounds kinda gross but—"

"Kinda gross?" Jolina squawked. "It sounds outright disgusting. I am absolutely *not* going to do that."

Being more of a science person than a math person, I had been truly fascinated by Ms. Carpenter's mini-science lesson on rigor mortis. And now that the image of Morty (flies and all) duct-taped to our poster board was out of my head, I focused on what Jonathan was saying.

Maybe I wanted to hang onto my newfound popularity. Maybe Morty really had become an instant legend to us students and I thought we owed him some sort of memorial. Most likely, I was desperate to get a good grade in math. For whatever reason, I was willing to try anything, and I found myself liking the Morty-on-the-poster idea.

"Hold on, Jolina. Calm down. I think Jonathan has a good idea," I said, soaking up the spewed lemonade on the carpet with the paper towels.

"You know," Aunt Willa chimed in, "last year in California, a truck carrying 1,600 pounds of saltwater bass to market got in a three-way crash. There's a group of people who want to have a memorial made for the fish that died."

"But if they were on their way to market, they were going to be killed anyway, right?" Jonathan said.

"Hey, I didn't say it made any sense," Aunt Willa replied and headed back down the hall.

"At least *this* idea does make sense," Jonathan said.

Lucille nodded. "Yeah, everyone knows about Morty, and half the school thinks he's some sort of hero for making the un-catchable catch."

"Maybe we could compromise." I looked to Jonathan and Lucille for support. "What about instead of doing time conversions on how long an animal's been dead, we focus on how long they live? We'll pick different animals, find out their average life spans, and do time conversions on that."

"Give me an example," Jolina said suspiciously.

Jonathan, seeing his chance to convince her about the memorial, jumped in. "Okay, well, let's say a possum, on average, lives two years. We'd do the math showing two years equals twenty-four months, or one hundred four weeks, and then break that down even more into days, hours, minutes, and seconds."

My mouth fell open in amazement at the speed Jonathan figured out how many weeks were in two years. Jolina had been telling me time conversions were easy, but everything was easy to her, so her opinion didn't really count. But Jonathan had just spit those numbers out faster than I could punch them into a calculator.

Lucille added her vote to the group. "Remember, Ms. Carpenter said creativity and originality are a big part of our grade. Let's face it, Jolina, this would make for a very interesting display. No one else would have anything even close to it."

Well, that sealed the deal. Jolina was as crazy about her grades as I was about order and cleanliness. In fact, the only time I'd ever seen her cry was when she got a B+ on a spelling test.

"Okay, fine." She tossed her hands up in surrender.

We spent the next hour coming up with a list of twelve different animals to compare. When it came time to divide them, Jolina took over.

"We'll each pick an animal and keep taking turns until we all have three animals to work with," she said.

Lucille nodded. "Good idea. I say Jonathan should go first since it was his idea to do this."

I closed my eyes and said a quick prayer that he would pick a huge animal. The way I saw it, the bigger the animal, the longer it probably lived—which meant less math. *I* planned on picking the smallest animals possible. Even though I usually want nothing to do with spiders, a black widow spider was on the list, and I wanted it. Anything that gets eaten by its mate can't have that long of a life span.

"I'll take the elephant for my first pick," said Jonathan.

"And I'll take the camel," Jolina said.

A sigh escaped my lips. Two big animals were off the list.

"I want the boa constrictor," said Lucille.

Drat! Along with the black widow, I also wanted the snake and box turtle.

Jolina kept track of everyone's picks, writing them down in her notebook.

She looked expectantly at me.

"The black widow," I said.

She raised her brow in surprise. "Really? You hate spiders."

"I've got my reasons."

We continued until we had picked all the animals. I ended up with the spider, the box turtle, and the Galapagos land tortoise.

I didn't know much about tortoises except they were related to turtles, and turtles were smallish, so the Galapagos land tortoise *must* be small, right? With logic like that, how could I go wrong?

CHAPTER ELEVEN
HYDROPLANE

hy·dro·plane
verb **hɪ**-drŏ-playn\

—to slide uncontrollably on a wet surface

Friday night, Lucille invited Jolina and me to a sleepover at her house. I loved going to Lucille's house because her mom was a way better cook than mine. Meatloaf was never served at Lucille's house.

Never.

I was also looking forward to not having to fight Chewy over my mattress and to finally getting a good night's sleep.

With my duffle bag slung over my shoulder and my pillow tucked under my arm, I headed down the street. I stopped at Jolina's house first and waited while she got her stuff together.

"Don't forget your makeup," I reminded her.

"It's already packed."

Lucille's mom didn't let her wear makeup so Jolina always brought hers. Mrs. O'Reilly said we could play with it, but not wear it outside.

We walked down to Lucille's and started with makeovers right away. When Lucille had finished mine, I looked in the mirror. She was great with hair, but I understood why her mom wasn't ready for her to start wearing makeup. Thanks to her, I looked like a circus clown.

Mrs. O'Reilly popped her head into Lucille's room. "Girls, dinner will be ready in—oh my. How . . . colorful you look, Ella."

Lucille looked pleased. "Thanks, Mom." She turned to me. "I told you it didn't look bad."

I kept quiet and looked back at Mrs. O'Reilly.

"What time did you say dinner was?" I asked, feeling my cheeks redden under all the rouge.

Mrs. O'Reilly shook her head as though to clear her vision. "I'd say in about ten minutes. Are you hungry for some manicotti?"

"Oh, I love your manicotti," I said, rubbing a tissue over my cheeks in an attempt to look normal at the dinner table.

Jolina pushed herself up from the floor and headed toward the door. "I'm ready to eat now if manicotti's on the menu."

Mrs. O'Reilly laughed. "You girls are sweet. I just took it out of the oven so give it a few minutes to cool." She went down the hall and we tidied up.

"Let's do mani-pedis after dinner," said Jolina.

"Sounds good to me," I said.

Lucille zipped Jolina's makeup bag shut. "I'm glad she made manicotti. That's one of the few things everyone in our family agrees on." Her four-year-old brother, Charlie, was the world's pickiest eater.

We all sat down at the dinner table and my stomach gurgled with anticipation. Everything smelled delicious. Mrs. O'Reilly had made two dishes of manicotti, a ginormous salad, and garlic bread that dripped with warm butter.

Charlie had a peanut butter and jelly sandwich on his plate along with his manicotti. He had a PB and J sandwich with every meal. It was his favorite food in the whole world.

"I made a cake today at my four school," Charlie announced to Jolina and me. The year before, Charlie had thought he was going to "three" school instead of preschool. So when he turned four, he naturally started saying he was going to four school.

Charlie was always coloring pictures of trains and superheroes for me. A few days earlier, he had said I was his best friend and if he ever had a pet rooster, he'd name it after me. So I knew he'd want me to be impressed with his cake announcement.

I flung my hand up to my chest in surprise like Mom would whenever Dad surprised her with flowers. "Amazing!" I said.

"You didn't *make* the cake, Charlie. You *decorated* it," Mrs. O'Reilly corrected. She turned to us. "They are learning about insects in his class and his teacher made each student a bumblebee cake. The kids got to decorate their own and bring it home. We'll all try some later."

"I named my cake Boogers," Charlie said proudly.

Mr. O'Reilly coughed into his water glass and Lucille snorted. Lucille adored Charlie and thought everything he said was funny.

"People don't name cakes, Charlie," said Mrs. O'Reilly, unfazed. "They eat them."

"We're going to *eat* my Boogers?" Charlie said.

Mr. O'Reilly hid his face in his napkin as his shoulders shook, and Lucille almost fell out of her chair laughing.

I'd been eating a ton of dark chocolate brownies lately and was not feeling any smarter. I was ready to try anything as long as it didn't have dark chocolate in it—even a cake named Boogers.

Mrs. O'Reilly raised her eyebrows at Charlie, who looked half-confused and half-delighted with his dad and sister's reactions. "You, young man, won't be having anything for dessert unless you eat all your dinner."

Charlie quietly concentrated on his meal after that.

We helped Mrs. O'Reilly clear the table, and she suggested we hang out upstairs for an hour before she served dessert.

Thirty minutes later, the three of us had cotton balls stuffed between our toes and were painting on nail polish.

"We should do this more often," I said. "Why can't school be this fun?"

Jolina repositioned her knee and leaned in closer toward her toes. "School is fun—most of the time. I just don't like it when Ms. Carpenter talks about gross stuff like rigor mortis."

Lucille laughed.

I grunted. "School is only fun for smart people."

"You're smart, Ella—you just need to change your perspective," said Jolina.

"You always sound like an adult—you know that, right?"

Jolina paused from her painting and looked up, grinning. "Thanks." She screwed the lid onto the bottle she held and set it down. "Seriously, though, don't let school get to you."

"I'm not going to let it get to me—in fact, I've got a plan." I painted my pinkie toe. Some nail polish got on my skin and I wiped it off before explaining my idea; I hated it when my pinkie toes looked larger than they really were. "I'm going to bribe Ms. Carpenter with a bag of Sour Patch Kids every day. She told me once they're her favorite."

"Isn't bribery illegal?" said Lucille.

I shrugged. "I'm still working out the kinks."

Jolina laughed. "Ella, you can't bribe Ms. Carpenter with candy so you'll get an A on the project."

I was about to respond when Mrs. O'Reilly came into the room and pretended to stagger toward the window. "Good grief, girls! The air in here is poisonous. Let's open a window, shall we?" She lifted the pane and took a deep breath. A kitchen towel was flopped over her shoulder and she took it off, using it to fan the smell of nail polish out the window.

"I wasn't trying to eavesdrop but I couldn't help overhearing your conversation." She sat down on Lucille's bed and put the towel next to her. "Personally, Ella, I would love it if someone gave me a bag of candy every day, but Jolina's right—you can't bribe your teacher." She cocked her head and raised her eyebrows at me. "Not that I actually thought you were going to do that anyway."

I smiled. "It seemed like a good idea."

"You can't control your circumstances, but you *can* control how you react to them."

"You moms all sound the same," I said. I knew she was right—but only about the bribery part. I was still sure there was a way I could control my circumstances and that I just hadn't found it yet.

Mrs. O'Reilly laughed and picked up the kitchen towel. "How about I bring in a couple cots and blankets? You don't have to set them up now, but you can if you want."

"That'd be great. Do you need help?" Jolina said.

"No, they're not heavy. I just need to see what Charlie is up to first—it's been too quiet for the last few minutes."

Charlie destroyed things in the O'Reilly household on a regular basis. Lucille said he didn't *mean* to ruin things; he was just curious about stuff. The bathroom was where he was usually the most destructive. Lucille kept a running tally of things he'd tried to flush down the toilet so far. We knew that Matchbox cars, LEGO bricks, and markers made it down, but the cowboy hat on his Woody doll and a full roll of toilet paper wouldn't.

Lucille was screwing the cap on her blue nail polish when we heard Mrs. O'Reilly from down the hall.

"No! No! No!"

We raced as fast as we could on our heels, making sure to keep our freshly painted toes up off the carpet. We looked like a horde of zombies with our funny waddle and our fingers spread out to keep from smearing our wet nails. Once we were in the hallway we were able to move faster; it was tile and not carpet, so we didn't need to walk on our heels. We sprinted down the hall toward the bathroom . . . which was not smart.

We found out later that Charlie had attached the vacuum cleaner extension hose to the bathroom faucet and left the other end hanging down. When he turned on the faucet, water poured out the door and down the hall, creating the world's first vacuum cleaner water slide. When our feet hit the wet floor the three of us put on a skating show that would have earned us an Olympic gold medal.

I landed with a splat and hydroplaned into the linen closet door. Jolina fell on top of me, and Lucille fell on top of Jolina.

Four hours later, I walked out of the emergency room with Mom, Dad, and a broken wrist. The bright pink cast on my right arm stopped just below my elbow. The nurse thought I got two black eyes from the fall as well until I explained that was just Lucille's attempt at doing my makeup.

We got home late—close to midnight. At least the next day was Saturday and I could sleep in. I whispered goodnight to Mom and Dad and, since Aunt Willa was sleeping, tiptoed into my room. Chewy was sacked out, snoring on my mattress again. I closed my eyes and gritted my teeth. Chewy was *one* situation I *was* going to control whether he liked it or not—I just wasn't sure how. I couldn't shove him off my bed before and I sure wouldn't be able to with a cast on.

Grabbing my pillow and blanket, I headed for the sofa, feeling sorry for myself. My wrist throbbed, I couldn't sleep in my own bed, and I never did get to eat any of Charlie's Booger cake.

CHAPTER TWELVE
BOMBSHELL

bomb·shell

noun **bom**-shel\

—something that comes as a great surprise

Each day, I realized more and more that Aunt Willa had turned into one disappointing roommate. I'd had certain expectations, and she hadn't met any of them. The hours of girl talk, a photography lesson or two, and a clean, organized room were all nonexistent. She didn't even draw anything cool on my cast—she just signed it.

Chewy still shoved me off the bed each night, but I decided to keep quiet about it. I figured sleeping on the sofa was better than listening to him bark all night if Aunt Willa put him outside. Mom and Dad didn't even know I was on the sofa— I usually was up and ready for school before either one of them ever made it out to the kitchen.

The biggest bummer, though, was the fact I was no longer allowed to use my own bathroom. Aunt Willa had completely taken it over with her photography junk. The chemicals she used for developing her photos stank to high heaven. She often tried to mask the stench by lighting a scented candle in the bedroom, but that made things smell even worse. The scent was called Sandalwood. Half the name was right. It smelled like sandals . . . sweaty gross ones.

On Sunday, I'd decided that another pedicure would be the perfect way to spend the afternoon. Friday night's slip-n-slide fiasco in the hallway had completely messed up the polish on my toes and I'd been wanting to redo them. Aunt Willa had gone to check on the renovations at her condo, so I stole a peek behind the heavy black curtain she'd hung in the bathroom doorway.

The nail polish collection I kept on the countertop was nowhere to be seen. I had a particularly complicated system for grouping my nail polish. It had taken me hours to come up with it and a whole Saturday to arrange all the bottles just right. The entire structure was based on color, whether or not there was glitter, and glow-in-the-dark ability. I had no idea where any of the bottles were, and I was pretty sure whoever moved the collection hadn't kept the bottles in the right order.

I walked into the kitchen and slumped down on a stool. Mom was pulling a sheet of dark chocolate chip cookies out of the oven.

"Why the sour face?" she said.

"Aunt Willa moved my nail polish and I don't know where it is," I said, picking at a piece of lint on my cast.

She shut the oven door and cocked her head. "What do you need your nail polish for?"

"I want to redo my nails since they got messed up Friday night. I'll be able to do it—I can still move my fingers," I said. I held up my right arm and wiggled my fingers around. "See?"

"It's probably under the sink or something. I wouldn't worry about it."

"But it took me forever to organize it all. I don't like it when people move my stuff," I muttered.

"Ella," Mom said. "It's nail polish. That's all."

"It's not *all*. It's the fact that my stuff got moved and nobody even asked me! My dresser's in my closet, my top two drawers were emptied out, I was kicked out of my own bed, I can't even use my bathroom, and now my nail polish is gone." I took a deep breath and continued. "Plus, I'm stuck listening to Aunt Willa's Peruvian panpipe music every time I walk into *my* room."

Mom chuckled.

"It's not funny."

Mom slid another cookie tray in the oven and then pulled out the stool next to me. "You're going to have to be flexible for the next few weeks, hon. I know you're used to having things done a certain way, but don't let pettiness get in the way of a good relationship."

"I'm not."

She raised her eyebrows.

"Okay, maybe just a little," I said.

"You need to process these feelings, Ella—don't keep them bottled up inside. Talk it out with your aunt and enjoy this time. You never know, you might learn something new." She handed me a warm cookie.

"Like what? How to move other people's stuff around and annoy them with weird music?" I replied.

She smacked me on the head with her potholder and stood up.

"No. More like just because you're an only child doesn't mean things will always go your way. I know Aunt Willa has her faults, but nobody's perfect."

I felt like she was treating me like one of her counseling clients again. I took my cookie and walked back to my room. Mom's words stung. I didn't *always* get my way. I just wanted things done a certain way. Surely I wasn't asking too much.

A couple hours later, Aunt Willa came into the room carrying a set of architectural plans under her arm. She plopped down on her bed and patted the spot next to her. "Want to see what I'm doing at the condo?"

I shrugged and walked over.

She shook the plans out of the tube and handed me one rolled end. She unfurled it and held onto the other side. Numbers, dimensions, symbols, and lines filled the page.

"Whoa," I said.

"I know this might look confusing, but I'll explain." She showed me her bedroom and where the walk-in closet was being built. Then she pointed to a double line in the kitchen. "See this wall here? It's going to be taken out so the kitchen can be enlarged."

"How big are you making it?" I asked.

"You tell me. See the dotted line here?" She pointed to the plans.

"Uh-huh."

"The dotted line is where the *new* wall will be. How do you find the area of something?"

"Really? You're giving me a math test right now?"

"It's not a test, goofy."

I sighed. "Fine. I think area is length times width."

"Good! Now look at the dimensions right here." She tapped the plans with her finger.

"Eleven by fifteen?" I said. "I multiply those two together, right?"

"Yep."

I stood and walked to my desk.

"Where are you going?" said Aunt Willa.

"To get a calculator." I opened the top drawer. "There's no way I can multiply that in my head." I plugged in the numbers. "One hundred and sixty-five square feet," I said.

"Bingo!" said Aunt Willa. "My current kitchen is only one hundred square feet so this will add a lot of extra space. You sure know your geometry."

"Geometry really isn't my strong point." I paused. "Actually, math in general isn't my strong point."

"That's okay. Your strengths lie in other areas. Not everyone was made to be a math whiz. But you still need to be able to handle everyday math."

"You don't use math," I argued, putting away my calculator. "That's one of the reasons I want to be a photographer. That, and I think it'd be a lot of fun to travel."

She laughed. "I use math all the time—*especially* when I'm traveling."

I spun around to face her. "What do you mean?"

"I have to estimate the weight of my baggage so I don't bring too much. There are different time zones to work with and various currencies to exchange. When I turn in expense reports, I have to make sure everything adds up to the right amount. I need to estimate distances correctly when I'm taking pictures to ensure I use the proper lens. And as I develop photographs, if I don't measure the amount of chemicals correctly, I could have a serious problem."

She rolled up the plans and stuffed them back in the tube. "You can't think of it as a test every time you do something math-related. You'll freak out if you do that. Anybody would."

I gripped the edge of my desk. "You sound like my mom."

"I'll take that as a compliment." She pushed herself off the bed. "I'm going to work in the darkroom for a bit." She placed her panpipe music in the CD player and disappeared behind the curtain, oblivious to the fact that she'd just destroyed my hopes of dodging the math bullet by becoming a photographer. I squeezed my eyes shut. Why do adults have to ruin everything?

CHAPTER THIRTEEN
MEATLOAF

meat·loaf
noun **meet**-lohf\

—ground meat molded into a loaf pan and baked;
often topped with brown sugar and ketchup

J ust when I thought things couldn't get worse,
rain poured throughout the afternoon, which
must have prompted Mom and Dad to decide
to start a weekly meatloaf night. Sundays were the
unlucky chosen night. Because of the rain, Chewy
was allowed to come inside early. He made himself

comfortable under the table and fell asleep. Since he wasn't disturbing anyone, Dad let him stay there when we sat down for dinner.

A ketchup-covered, grayish-brown slab of meatloaf the size of Texas was plopped onto my plate, along with some mac and cheese and green beans. I felt a nudge against my leg.

I looked down.

Chewy looked up.

His eyes begged for meaty goodness. I thought of telling him that meaty goodness did *not* exist at the table that night, but then I had a brilliant idea.

I scanned the table as I stabbed a piece of meatloaf with my fork. When no one was looking, I plucked it off and gave it to Chewy. He licked my fingers clean. No one noticed. I cut off two more pieces, each a little bigger. I quickly slid them one at a time under the table. They disappeared in seconds. My plan was working. The meatloaf was now about the size of Arkansas, but I knew Mom and Dad would get suspicious if they saw it was disappearing faster than usual. I pushed some green beans around my plate for a while and took a couple bites of mac and cheese.

I glanced over at Aunt Willa. Most of her meatloaf was gone already! Apparently she really missed it while in Africa. She seemed tired, too. I lost track of the number of times she dropped her napkin and reached down to pick it up.

I stuffed in a couple more mouthfuls of mac and cheese. Half the meatloaf was still on my plate. I figured Chewy could handle what was left in a single swallow. The question was how to get such a large bite to him without being caught. Desperate times called for desperate measures. I knocked my water glass over, sending a pool of liquid across the table toward Mom.

"Oops!" I grabbed my glass and stood it up-right.

"It's okay. I'll grab a towel." Mom pushed her chair back and went to the kitchen. Dad mopped up water as best he could with his napkin. I looked at Aunt Willa. She dropped her napkin again. Poor thing.

I quickly grabbed the remaining chunk of meatloaf and shoved it under the table. With a slurp and a lick, it was gone. Chewy's soft tongue cleaned every drop of ketchupy sauce off my hand.

Mom came back from the kitchen with the towel.

"Thanks, Mom. I guess I'm not used to this cast yet." I took the towel from her and cleaned up the remaining water. "I'm going to grab something to drink."

Aunt Willa pushed back her chair. "I'll come with you. I need some more, too."

She followed me to the kitchen. "I've always referred to your mom's meatloaf as 'the mystery meatbrick'!" she whispered over my shoulder as I turned on the faucet.

I busted out laughing. "That's perfect! That's what I'm going to call it from now on."

"Of all the foods I miss when I travel, meatloaf never makes the list. I just didn't want to tell your mom. She and your dad are so fond of it."

So was Chewy, apparently.

"And now we get to have it every Sunday night," I muttered. "Yippee."

"Well, at least Chewy liked it."

I winced. "You saw me?"

"Saw you? I was talking about *me*."

My mouth dropped open. "You fed yours to Chewy, too?"

She giggled and nodded. "Why do you think I kept dropping my napkin?"

"Oh man. I thought only kids snuck food to dogs under the table."

"Well, maybe I'm a kid at heart." She winked and walked back to the dining room.

I smiled and shook my head. We weren't having girl talk exactly, but she was my partner in crime when it came to getting rid of meatloaf, and that was worth something. I was going to have to give Aunt Willa another chance.

Later that night, I draped my favorite pair of jeans over my desk chair for school the next morning and went to Mom to have her wrap my arm in a plastic bag so I could take a shower. The doctor had said the cast couldn't get wet for the next six weeks. I came back thirty minutes later with a towel wrapped around my head and another around my body.

Chewy stood on my mattress with his jaws clamped down on my jeans, growling and whipping his head side to side.

"No, Chewy!" I held my towel in place with my cast and grabbed a book from my desk with the other hand. I whacked the book several times on the desk, hoping it would startle him into dropping the pants. "Let go!"

He struck a playful pose. I grabbed at the jeans and yanked. "I'm not playing with you, you dumb dog. Let go of them!"

Aunt Willa rushed into the room. "Chewy! Drop it!"

Chewy sat and lowered his head, dropping my jeans. But before I could yank them away, he made a hacking sound and up came two helpings of meatloaf.

I felt my eyes widen in horror as I backed into Aunt Willa. "Oh no! Not on my jeans!" I moaned.

"Oh, honey, I'm so sorry," Aunt Willa said, looking at the jeans. "I'll wash them right now. Maybe they won't stain."

She gathered them up so the vomit wouldn't slide off and carefully carried them out of the room. Chewy whined and wobbled over to my mattress. It was hard to feel sorry for that brute after he barfed all over my favorite pair of jeans, but he did look pretty pitiful lying there. Mom's meatloaf had struck again.

CHAPTER FOURTEEN

CONVERT

con·vert

verb \kŏn-**vurt**\

—to change from one form or character
or use to another

The math fair was scheduled for the end of the week. The preparations took up our entire math time on Monday and even a little bit of our art class since the art teacher helped us with poster designs. That afternoon, Jonathan and Lucille stayed in the classroom to discuss the layout for our booth. Ms. Carpenter gave Jolina and me permission to go to the library to finish doing research on our animals.

I discovered that while Galapagos land tortoises *are* related to turtles, they're *not* small. They're the size of a dishwasher. Okay, maybe not that big, but close. And it turned out both the box turtle and the tortoise could live well over a hundred years!

Mega-disappointing.

Thank goodness black widows ate each other and didn't live long. I looked at my paper. The average black widow lived about one year.

Jonathan had made charts for each of us to fill out for every animal. It had spaces for writing in how many years, months, weeks, days, hours, minutes, and seconds the animal lived. I gripped my pencil the best I could and felt like a kinder-gartener learning how to write for the first time. The cast made my usually tidy and precise writing look like scribble-scrabble.

I sloppily wrote a 1 in the year column, a 12 in the months, 52 in the weeks, and then 365 for the days. After that, I stopped and turned to Jo-lina. "That part was easy—but now I've got to convert the days to hours and stuff. How do I do that?"

"Did you bring your calculator?" she said. "You're going to need it. These numbers get big fast, and it's really hard for people to do this in their heads."

I reached into my backpack and dug out my calculator.

"Okay," said Jolina, pushing her own animal calculations aside. She looked at my printout. "You know a black widow lives for three hundred and sixty-five days. How many hours are in one day?"

"Twenty-four."

"Right, so if twenty-four hours are in one day, and you have three hundred and sixty-five days, what should you do?"

"I multiply them?"

"Yep," Jolina said. "If you have three hundred and sixty-five sets of twenty-four hours, you have how many hours?"

I plugged the numbers into my calculator as Jolina watched. "A black widow lives for eight thousand seven hundred and sixty hours."

"You got it. Now to solve for minutes, it's the same process. How many minutes are in one hour?"

"Sixty."

"Umm-hmm. So if you have eight thousand seven hundred and sixty hours and you know that sixty minutes are in one hour . . ." She didn't finish her sentence; instead, she looked at me with her eyebrows raised.

"I multiply eight thousand seven hundred and sixty hours by sixty minutes?"

"See. You know what you're doing."

"Hold up—we aren't done yet," I said, punching those numbers in. "It's five hundred and twenty-five thousand, six hundred minutes in all."

Jolina moved her papers back in front of her and picked up her pencil. "I think you know what you're doing. You just have to figure out the seconds now."

"So I would multiply the minutes by sixty again, because there are sixty seconds in a minute, right?"

"Right."

"I can see why we celebrate years on birthday cakes instead of minutes. Can you imagine trying to light five hundred and twenty-five thousand, six hundred candles?" I said, imagining my mom running around the kitchen armed with a fire extinguisher.

Last year, Mom had bought trick candles for Dad's birthday cake—the kind that you can't blow out. She forgot to dip them in water afterward and one lit up again, re-igniting the others. Luckily, Dad saw what happened and threw the plate of burning candles into the sink, but not before the roll of paper towels went up in flames. After that, Mom kept a fire extinguisher under the sink.

"Mom would need to whip out her fire extinguisher if we put candles on our cakes for every minute we lived instead of every year. Our whole house would catch fire."

Jolina snickered. "It'd be just one more disaster in a long line of them at your house, huh?" I'd already filled her in on how Chewy was leaving a path of destruction that was wider than Lucille's little brother Charlie was even capable of.

She raised her eyebrows and nodded. Like me, Jolina liked things clean and organized. She understood the frustration I was feeling because of Aunt Willa and Chewy.

Mrs. Gottry, the media specialist, walked to our table and leaned over us. We were the only ones in the library, but she still whispered—I don't think she knew how to talk otherwise. "Do you girls have everything you need? Is your project coming along well?"

Jolina looked up. "Yes, ma'am—we're just working on some conversions now."

I quickly punched numbers into my calculator. "Did you know a black widow can live for thirty-one million, five hundred and thirty-six thousand seconds?" I said to Mrs. Gottry.

She peered over her glasses. "Can it now? Well, I must admit I didn't know that. Quite fascinating. What other animals do you have, dear?"

I set the black widow sheet aside and picked up my other two. "I have a box turtle and the Galapagos land tortoise."

"Oh my—those live for ages. You'll have fun with those calculations."

"How is it everyone except me knew that turtles and tortoises lived forever?" I asked once she'd walked away.

Jolina shrugged. "We tried to tell you."

Oddly enough, at the end of the day I didn't feel so anxious about all the math that was necessary for our project. Maybe Mom's advice about viewing math through the eyes of a scientist worked after all. In this particular case, all my math problems really were science-related, and I actually was looking forward to working on them. That would never have happened if not for Morty.

At least his death was not in vain.

CHAPTER FIFTEEN

CLOSE SHAVE

close shave

noun \klohz shayv\

—something achieved (or escaped)
by a narrow margin

After school on Tuesday, Jonathan, Lucille, Jolina, and I met once more, this time at Jonathan's house, to finalize plans for our display and to divide out jobs for getting everything done.

"I have a special prop I'll bring in on Thursday," said Jolina.

"What is it?" said Jonathan.

"It's a secret. But I know you're gonna love it!"

"I want to do the display layout," Lucille said, bouncing on her toes. "I love doing artsy stuff. Just give me the spreadsheets and photographs and I'll put everything together."

A wave of panic flooded over me. The thought of Lucille putting our display together made me break out in a cold sweat. Her artwork was not a lot better than her work with eye shadow. And she wasn't exactly what I would call the world's greatest speller. She'd even misspelled the word "spelling" on our last vocab test. Plus, if I was crazy clean and organized, she was the polar opposite: crazy sloppy and cluttered. I knew this was supposed to be a group project, but I couldn't see how letting Lucille misspell half the words on our display board would be helpful to anyone—especially me. My math grade and summer depended on a *perfect* display.

I looked over at Jolina and Jonathan, pleading with my eyes for them to realize the danger in handing over the poster to Lucille, but they seemed oblivious to the fact that she could destroy everything we'd worked so hard on.

I would need to talk to Lucille later.

Jolina picked up the calculations we'd all done for the animal life spans and looked at Jonathan and me. "We need these turned into spreadsheets and we also need pictures of the different animals to place near each one."

"I'll print out the pictures," Jonathan and I said at the same time. We looked at each other.

"Rock, Paper, Scissors?" he said.

"No way. I'm the world's biggest loser with Rock, Paper, Scissors. I'm sure not about to gamble with that game."

"I'll shoot ya for it," Jonathan said.

"Excuse me?"

"Basketball," he said. "I challenge you to a game of HORSE. The loser has to do the spreadsheets."

"Come on! Her arm's in a cast—she can't play basketball," Lucille said.

Like heck I couldn't.

I narrowed my eyes and looked at him. "Are you good at basketball?"

He grinned. "Maybe."

I thought back to when we first went to his house. I'd passed his room on my way to the bathroom and poked my head in to see what a boy's room looked like—not having any siblings, I was curious. I remembered a large GO ARMY flag was pinned above his bed and his walls were plastered with all kinds of basketball posters. He also had a basketball laundry hamper—the kind where you shoot your dirty clothes through a hoop and into the basket. There were clothes all over the floor, so he was either really sloppy or a really bad basketball player. Considering he was part of a military family, I couldn't see him being sloppy.

While I wasn't the greatest athlete, my dad and I had shot hoops since I could walk. True, I did have a cast on and my shots might look ugly, but if I could avoid doing the math spreadsheets, it would be worth any potential humiliation on the court. "You're on."

"You sure?" Jonathan asked. "I was partly kidding . . . I don't want you to hurt your arm or anything."

"I'll be fine," I said.

"I'll referee," Lucille offered.

We finished off a bag of cheese puffs and went outside. By the time Jolina had to go home, I had

H, O, and R. Jonathan had H, O, R, and S. The
funny thing was that I was actually shooting better
than I normally did. Because my right arm was in
a cast, I was forced to really concentrate and slow
down before each shot.

"Get him out, Ella!" Jolina called over her
shoulder as she left.

"Not likely," said Jonathan, squaring off for
a shot. He lobbed the ball high and swooshed it
through the net. "I'm planning on getting a basketball scholarship."

"No problem," I sneered, dribbling the ball
back to where he'd shot from.

I missed.

"Ha!" Jonathan said. "We're tied. Now, who's
going down first?"

I tossed him the ball. "Take your best shot,
Johnny-basketball."

He walked to the end of his driveway and stood
next to his mailbox. "You have to shoot from back
here."

"Only if *you* make it," I reminded him.

"Oh, I'll make it." He judged the distance and
heaved the ball through the air. It ricocheted off
the backboard and flew into Lucille's yard.

Lucille and I turned and busted out laughing as Jonathan ran to retrieve his ball. He came back smiling and tossed it to me. "Let's see what *you've* got."

Like I always say, desperate times called for desperate measures. It looked as though I would have to pull out the "hop n' hook it." Whenever Dad and I needed a break from "real" basketball, we'd make up silly shots. I knew I'd risk looking ridiculous in front of Jonathan doing it, but hopefully I could get him out.

"Okay. You have to hop in a circle three times on one foot and then throw a left handed hook shot." I began bouncing on my right foot.

"What kind of shot is that?" Jonathan taunted.

"A you-can't-make-it kind," I replied as I released the ball into the air. It circled around the rim and dropped through the net.

Jonathan's head tipped back. "Aww, man!" He dribbled the ball a couple times and wobbled on one foot. He bounced awkwardly around in a circle three times and tossed the ball toward the hoop. At least I assumed that's what he was aiming for since it hit nothing but air.

Lucille jumped up and cheered. I slapped her a high-five. Jonathan walked over with the ball tucked under his arm. "I can't believe I just got beat in basketball by a girl with a broken arm." He grinned and shook his head. "I'll have to try to take my dad out using that shot. I'm pretty sure he's *never* bounced on one foot in a circle before shooting."

Lucille's mom poked her head out of her front door. "Lucille, time to come in. We have to leave for your sister's piano recital soon."

"I better head home, too," I said. "Have fun with those spreadsheets, Jonathan!"

He pretended to belly laugh and slapped his knee. "Haha—you're so funny. Just make sure everyone has their calculations to me by tomorrow."

"I'll do you a favor—I'll call Jolina and Lucille to tell them. I love being helpful," I joked.

CHAPTER SIXTEEN

SPREADSHEET

spread·sheet

noun **spred**-sheet\\

—a computer program that calculates numbers
and organizes information in columns and rows

Just before school let out on Wednesday, we all
gave Jonathan our life span calculations so he
could create the spreadsheets.

Around four o'clock, the phone rang at home.
It was Jonathan. "You're not gonna believe this."

"What?" I said.

"Our computer just crashed. Blue screen of death and all."

"Are you kidding me?"

"I'm dead serious. My mom's on the phone with tech support right now, but I'm pretty sure it's trashed."

"Oh no. That's terrible."

"Yeah, it's not the greatest timing. My dad's got this military dinner thing we have to go to, and I really need to get this done before we leave. I ran over to Lucille's to see if I could use their computer, but no one was home."

"Yeah—she has Girl Scouts on Wednesday. Let me check with Mom, but I'm sure you can come on over to my house and use ours." I cupped my hand over the receiver and told Mom about Jonathan's computer. "She said to come on over."

"Great, thanks! I'll be there in a few minutes," Jonathan said.

He arrived with his backpack swung over one shoulder just as I finished printing out the last of the animal photos. "I'm going to grab some construction paper to glue these to. The laptop is in the living room on the coffee table—I'll meet you there in a second."

"Awesome," said Jonathan, pulling the papers with our calculations out of his backpack. He spent close to an hour rearranging columns and rows, entering numbers, and working with different fonts for each sheet.

Every once in a while, I'd peek over his shoulder to make sure it looked good. After the tenth time, he crossed his arms and tapped his foot. "Can I help you with something?"

My shoulders slumped. "Sorry—I just want it to be perfect."

"You worry too much. It'll look great." He checked the time on his watch.

"What time do you have to leave for your dad's dinner?" I said.

"At eighteen-hundred hours."

I looked up from my gluing. "When?"

He grinned. "Habit, sorry. Everything at our house is told in military time."

"I don't know how to tell military time."

"It's easy. Just add twelve to any time after twelve noon, and you'll know what time it is. One o'clock in the afternoon is one plus twelve, or thirteen-hundred hours. Two o'clock in the afternoon is two plus twelve, or fourteen-hundred hours."

I did the math in my head. Backwards. "So eighteen-hundred is eighteen minus twelve? It's really six o'clock?"

"Yep." He leaned back on the sofa and sighed. "Okay, I think I'm done. Should I print it out?"

"Yeah, go for it. I think the printer is still on."

He walked over to the printer to get his papers. Picking them up, he gave a nod of approval. "Perfect." He grinned. "*Now* do you want to see them? I'm gonna start packing up."

"Sure." I put down the glue bottle and Jonathan handed me the spreadsheets—one for each animal. "Wow," I said. "There sure are a lot of numbers on these."

He let out a small laugh. "Yeah, well, the animals we picked live for a ton of minutes and seconds."

"You're telling me—I'm the one who had to figure out the tortoise, remember? I didn't know a calculator could show that many numbers."

He started to put the spreadsheets in his bag, but I stopped him. "Why don't you leave the spreadsheets here? I'll put them with the photos and give them to Lucille at the back gate tomorrow morning."

"You sure?"

"Yeah. We might as well keep everything together," I said, knowing full well that I wasn't planning on giving anything to Lucille.

He shrugged. "Okay." He handed me the papers and I put them on top of the photos I'd printed.

"Thanks again for letting me come over and use your computer. I wasn't sure what I was going to do when Mom told me ours had kicked the bucket."

I grimaced. "I remember when our last computer crashed. My mom cried for hours because there were some photos she hadn't saved to the external hard drive and they were gone forever." I looked over at the closed laptop. "Speaking of saving stuff, what name did you save the spreadsheets under?"

"I've got them saved on my thumb drive." He pulled the thumb drive from his pocket. "Do you want to hold onto it, just in case?"

I shrugged. "Sure, but you checked everything, right?"

"Yep. Several times."

He handed me the thumb drive. It was shaped like the Incredible Hulk. I pulled off the Hulk's legs to reveal the metal part that plugs into the USB port. "That's cool."

"Thanks—my dad gave it to me for my birthday last year."

I stuck the Hulk's legs back on and set the thumb drive on the table. "I think we're done for now."

"Sounds good. I'll see you tomorrow."

Jonathan headed home and I finished gluing the printed photos of animals onto construction paper. I put the spreadsheets in a pile, placed the photographs and thumb drive on top, and carried the stack to my room, where I placed it on top of my book bag on the floor. I didn't want to put them inside my bag because the glue still needed to dry. But I quickly picked them up again. With Chewy eating half my belongings and barfing on the other half, I didn't want these anywhere he'd be able to reach. They needed to be kept somewhere high off the floor.

I opened the closet door, thinking the dresser would be a great spot, but Aunt Willa's stuff covered every inch of the top. I could put them in Mom's office, but not until she was done for the day. She had a strict rule about people walking in and out of her office during "work hours."

Frustrated, I sighed and wished for the hundredth time that Chewy (and Aunt Willa) had stayed at someone else's house. I glanced at the clock. Chewy wasn't even allowed inside until after dinner, so I could safely leave the papers on my backpack to dry until after my shower. Then, I figured, I'd stash everything in Mom's office where it'd be safe until morning.

Tomorrow was Thursday—just one more day of prep and then the math fair. Just one more day until I would know the fate of my summer. If only something would tip the scales in my favor.

I hoped Lucille was home by now because I needed to call her . . . and let her know that I would be taking over her job as display designer.

CHAPTER SEVENTEEN
SELF-INTEREST

self·in·ter·est
noun **self-in**-tĕ-rist\

—regard for one's own interest or advantage,
especially with disregard for others

I grabbed the phone in the kitchen and went out to the front porch. I didn't want my parents hearing my conversation; I knew they wouldn't understand and they'd probably think I was being mean. But seriously, Lucille was horrible with vocabulary and spelling, and she was sloppy. It was *my* grade hanging in the balance, not just hers. I swatted at a mosquito buzzing near my face, and the stub of a pencil I'd stuck behind my ear earlier fell to the driveway. I picked it up and started fidgeting with it between my fingers nervously. After pacing for a few minutes, I dialed Lucille's number.

Mrs. O'Reilly picked up on the second ring. "Hello?"

"Hi Mrs. O'Reilly. It's Ella. Can I speak with Lucille?"

"Sure, hon. Hold on."

A few seconds later, Lucille picked up. "Hey. What's up?"

I eased into the conversation. "How was Girl Scouts?"

"Great! I got my first-aider level 1 badge."

"That's cool." I took a deep breath. "So, I've been thinking about the layout for the math project."

"Me, too! I'm so excited to work on it. Did you and Jonathan get everything printed out?"

I filled her in on Jonathan's computer crash as I continued to pace back and forth in our driveway.

"I'm glad you were home, Ella. Can you imagine if he came to school tomorrow without the stuff to give me?"

"Yeah, about that." A pit formed in my stomach. "I think I should probably do the layout."

There was a pause. "But why? That's my job."

"I know," I said, "but . . . umm . . . it has to be— it's really important that it looks . . . well . . . perfect."

"What do you mean? I'll do a good job."

"Let's face it, Lucille—you're not a great speller, and you're really messy. You can't even find your homework half the time because it's crumpled up in the bottom of your backpack. I don't want to fail because of you." I closed my eyes and grimaced, ashamed of what I had just said. It hadn't come out right at all.

There was dead silence on the other end.

"Lucille?"

She sniffled. "What?"

"I'm sorry. I didn't mean that." I sighed. "I meant that my math grade is so bad right now that if I don't get a hundred percent on this project, I'm doomed. I just want to do everything I can to make sure I get an A plus."

"What am I supposed to do, then? Everything else has been done."

I looked at the pencil I held. "How about you bring in a bunch of pencils and paper for people to use when they visit the booth?"

"Pencils and paper?"

"Yeah, and calculators." I tried to sound excited, like it was a great idea or something, but it sounded pretty lame to me. "Please, Lucille, I know I can be a control freak sometimes, but this is really important to me."

I could hear a long sigh on the other end. I knew I had hurt her feelings. "Are you mad at me?"

"Sort of," she said. "But I'll get over it."

That was the thing about Lucille—she didn't hold grudges. I knew I was taking advantage of that, but I felt I had no choice.

"Thanks, Lucille. I'll see you tomorrow at the back gate, okay?"

"Okay," she mumbled.

I put the phone back in the kitchen and rubbed my temples. I had a headache and the skin underneath my cast itched like crazy. I jabbed the tiny pencil between my arm and the cast and scratched it the best I could.

It felt *fantastic*.

Until I lost my grip on the pencil.

I pushed my fingers down as far as I could, desperately trying to feel for the eraser tip, but I couldn't reach it. I leaned my head against the wall and sighed.

I needed longer fingers.

And I needed to move to a planet where there were no math fairs, sloppy friends, itchy casts, and short pencils.

I headed toward my bedroom, ready for the day to be over . . . and ready to get those papers off my floor. It was close to dinnertime and Mom was about to finish in her office.

I froze in horror when I reached my doorway.

CHAPTER EIGHTEEN
LAST STRAW

last straw

noun \last straw\

—unacceptable, beyond bearing

"Nooooo!" I screamed.

Chewy's legs scrambled under him so fast he had a hard time moving. He shot out of my room, knowing full well he did not want me to catch him.

"Get back here, you dumb dog! You're going to wish you never set a paw in this house!" I screeched.

I chased him down the hallway, flattening Aunt Willa and Mom against the wall as they hurried toward my room.

"Ella!" Mom said. "What's going on? What happened?"

I turned around to face Mom. Tears welled up in my eyes. "*This* is what happened!" I cried. I thrust the half-eaten, torn spreadsheets and photographs in her face.

Aunt Willa gasped and Mom's hand flew to her mouth. "Oh no!"

"I think he ate Jonathan's thumb drive, too. And it was a birthday present from his dad!" I glared at Aunt Willa. "What's he doing inside? He's not supposed to come in this early!"

"Oh honey . . . I . . . I let him inside so I could give him his heartworm medicine. He went and laid down afterward, and I thought he went to sleep. I am so sorry."

"We're supposed to put our displays together tomorrow! I'm going to fail because of your mangy mutt!" I knew I was yelling, but I couldn't stop. Something inside me exploded and the words just kept coming. "He's ruined my favorite pair of jeans, and he's kicked me out of bed every night since you got here so I'm stuck sleeping on the sofa! *You've* moved all my stuff so I can't find it and you've taken over my bathroom with all your photography junk. I *hate* the smell of your candle and can't stand your music!"

I couldn't see anything through my tears, but I heard Aunt Willa gasp.

"Ella!" Mom's voice cut in sharply.

I stood there, shoulders shaking, and sobbed.

I was mad.

Mad at Chewy.

Mad at Aunt Willa.

Mad at math.

Mad at the fact photographers had to *do* math.

Mom must have sensed what I was feeling because she pulled me toward her and simply wrapped her arms around me. She held me tight until I ran out of tears. When I looked up, I saw Aunt Willa. She stood rubbing her arms and shifting her weight back and forth on her feet.

"Ella," she said quietly. "I am *so* sorry about the spreadsheets. And the jeans. And that Chewy took over your bed. You're up and ready for school before I'm awake so I didn't know he'd been doing that. As for Jonathan's thumb drive, I don't really know what to do about that." She leaned over and tucked a strand of hair behind my ear. "And I'm doubly sorry I hid your stuff on you. I didn't mean to—I just forgot to tell you where I was putting things. I didn't realize you didn't like the candle or the music. Do you forgive me?"

What was I supposed to say with Mom standing right there? At least she hadn't interrupted with a speech on the importance of "processing feelings through open communication." However, I knew Mom would say I owed Aunt Willa an apology for my outburst. I sniffed and nodded that I forgave her—but I didn't really mean it. "I'm sorry I yelled at you."

Mom raised her eyebrows.

"Sometimes I'm overly picky about my room. And it's not *your* fault that Chewy eats everything in sight and is a—"

Mom cleared her throat.

"—never mind," I muttered.

Aunt Willa took the destroyed spreadsheets from Mom's hand. She looked them over and shook her head. "I'm going to make this up to you, Ella. I'll help you redo this, and it will be good as new. We'll stay up all night if we have to." She smiled. "Maybe we can even manage to keep Chewy off your bed."

I snickered, but because of my runny nose, it came out more like a snort. Hearing his name, Chewy peeked around the hall and warily walked toward us.

"It's all right, Chewy," I said. "I won't chase you down the hall again."

Mom glanced at her watch. "It's almost time for me to start dinner. Should I just bring you two something to munch on in your room so you can keep working?"

"Good idea," said Aunt Willa.

"Meatloaf sandwiches?" Mom suggested.

"No!" we quickly said. At the mere mention of meatloaf, poor Chewy whined and ran back down the hall. Aunt Willa and I looked at each other, and despite my anger, I couldn't help but smile a little.

"I'll tell you what," Aunt Willa said. "How about I order us a pizza? I'll get one for your parents and one just for us."

I wiped my nose with my sleeve. "Pepperoni and pineapple?" I said.

She winked. "Is there any other way to have pizza?"

Mom put Chewy outside while Aunt Willa ordered the pizzas. I grabbed the laptop from off the coffee table and we locked ourselves in my room to work.

"I hope nothing else was on Jonathan's thumb drive. I don't know how I'm going to tell him the Incredible Hulk is being digested."

Aunt Willa bit her lip. "Chewy has a stomach made of steel, but I hope that doesn't make him sick."

I thought for a minute and then, feeling slightly vengeful, I smiled. "You know, he threw up after eating Mom's meatbrick." I raised my eyebrows and looked at Aunt Willa.

Her eyes widened as my comment sank in. "Are you suggesting we feed him some more and hope he throws up again?"

I nodded. "Seems like a good use of Mom's meatloaf to me, and maybe it will teach Chewy not to swallow everything in sight."

Operation Dog Puke was put in motion. I snuck a slice of meatloaf out of the kitchen and met Aunt Willa in the backyard. At first, Chewy wouldn't touch it. He must have remembered what happened last time. I figured maybe if I squirted a bunch of ketchup on it, he might eat up. Half a bottle of ketchup later, he licked the plate clean. Ten minutes later, Aunt Willa, Chewy, and I stared down at the Incredible Hulk swimming in a blob of brown and red pure nastiness.

Aunt Willa grimaced. "Tell Jonathan I'll get him a new thumb drive."

CHAPTER NINETEEN
REALITY

re·al·i·ty

noun \ree-**al**-i-tee\

—something that exists or that is real

While we waited for the pizza to arrive, I explained to Aunt Willa what I wanted the spreadsheets to look like. I tried to show her the old ones, but Chewy's handiwork made it next to impossible and nothing was retrievable from the thumb drive. I still had everyone's calculations on their animals, thankfully.

I sent up a quick hallelujah that I hadn't thrown those out after Jonathan had finished. The last thing I wanted was to be stuck redoing *everyone's* time conversions. We turned on the computer and pulled up a spreadsheet.

"I know this program," Aunt Willa said. "I use it for my budgeting." She turned to me and winked. "More math in real life. We can bust out this project in no time."

I breathed a sigh of relief. As much fun as it would have been to pull an all-nighter with Aunt Willa, I was actually looking forward to sleeping on my mattress. Aunt Willa had already told me Chewy would be fine outside for the night.

"Pizza guy is at the door!" Mom hollered down the hall.

"I'm coming!" said Aunt Willa. She turned to me. "Start inputting these numbers here." She pointed to a column. "I'll be right back." She disappeared out the door as I sat at my desk and got to work.

Aunt Willa returned with our pizza and two cans of soda.

An hour and a half later, we looked over the freshly printed charts of each animal's life span.

Aunt Willa had shown me some things on the computer program I hadn't known about before. The spreadsheets looked better now than before Chewy had eaten them. Apparently, Chewy was a blessing in disguise when it came to both meat-loaf and math homework.

"All I need now is to go online and print out pictures of the animals on the chart," I said.

"Hold that thought," Aunt Willa said as she removed the pizza box from the desk. She ducked behind the darkroom curtain and returned with a stack of photos in her hand. "The reason I didn't want you to go into your bathroom lately was because I wanted these to be a surprise." She set a pile of photographs on the desk and gently slid them over. I spread them out. Beautiful, glossy, full-sized images of lions, elephants, hippos, and other animals from her trip to Africa appeared in front of me. "When you told me what your math fair team decided to do for a display, I thought it was . . . well, brilliant. And when you told me what animals you'd picked, I was so excited because I *knew* I had these photos—I just needed to develop the film. Some of these photographs are from other trips, like the platypus, but I had the negatives back at the condo."

"They're beautiful." I felt a twinge of guilt for being angry she'd taken over my bathroom. After all, she'd done it so she could do something nice for me.

She pulled out the elephant photograph and laid it on top. "I remember this elephant in particular. She had a young calf with her who was absolutely adorable. Just loved to play in water."

I picked up the elephant photo. "You know, Aunt Willa, you kinda burst my bubble when you told me all the math you have to use with photography."

"Sorry about that. But you need to reset your expectations, Ella Bella. The reality is there's not a job out there that doesn't use math. Some use it more than others, but it's everywhere." She gave my shoulders a squeeze. "The good news is, I know you can do it."

I was quiet for a minute or two as I examined her photos. "It must be fun to take pictures for a living."

She sat on the bed and fluffed the pillow. "It is and it isn't. Sometimes the pictures I take aren't fun at all. Sometimes they're of very sad and tragic things like war, famine, and other injustices."

"Why do you photograph stuff like that?" I asked.

"Well, just because you don't like something doesn't mean you can ignore it and hope it goes away." She leaned against her pillow. "One of my favorite quotes is by Edmund Burke. He said, 'All it takes for evil to succeed is for good men to do nothing.' Part of my job is to help make good people aware of evil and injustices so they can do something about it."

It was close to ten o'clock by the time we finished and cleaned up everything. Between the crying and staring at a computer screen, my eyes felt like sandpaper. As I closed them to try to sleep, I thought about Aunt Willa's favorite quote. I kept hearing her voice: *just because you don't like something doesn't mean you can ignore it and hope it goes away.* Her words struck a chord with me. It wasn't the girl talk I'd imagined we'd have when I first learned she'd be staying with me, but it felt more important. Even though I was still a little mad at her, I was glad she was around.

CHAPTER TWENTY

APPREHENSION

ap·pre·hen·sion

noun \ap-ri-**hen**-shŏn\

—fearful expectation or anticipation

The next morning at the playground, I pulled Jonathan aside. "There's something I need to tell you." I hung my head and rearranged the gravel with my shoes.

"What?"

"Chewy ate your thumb drive," I said and then bit my lip.

"He what?"

"He ate your thumb drive," I repeated. "But we got him to throw it up again by feeding him my mom's meatloaf."

Jonathan's face contorted to an odd combination of amusement and shock.

"My aunt ordered another Incredible Hulk thumb drive last night to replace yours—but please tell me there wasn't anything else on it besides the spreadsheets."

He thought for a minute and then shook his head. "Nope. This was my first school project since I got it."

I breathed a sigh of relief. "I am so sorry, Jonathan. That dumb dog eats *everything*."

"Don't worry about it," he said. "I think it's funny you fed him your mom's meatloaf to make him throw up."

"You haven't tried it," I said.

He laughed and started to walk off.

I grabbed his arm. "Wait. That's not all."

Jonathan raised his eyebrows.

"He ate the spreadsheets, too."

"But they were saved on the thumb—"

I put both hands up. "It's okay. My aunt and I redid them. I just didn't want you wondering why the spreadsheets I had today weren't the ones *you* did yesterday."

He shrugged. "As long as we have them, I don't care who did them."

"Thanks for being so nice about the whole thumb drive and spreadsheet mess."

He smiled. "No problem."

The bell rang for the start of the day and we headed to Ms. Carpenter's room. During math time, as the class assembled their projects, Ms. Carpenter told us both our principal, Mr. Morris, and the librarian, Mrs. Gottry, were going to be the judges. "They will choose one Best of Show project from the whole fifth grade. Everyone in the winning group will receive a trophy and a free ice cream sundae at Peghiny's Ice Cream Parlor," Ms. Carpenter said.

Peghiny's Ice Cream was the best in the world. They had some of the craziest flavors I'd ever heard of, like Pink Mud Pie, Alien Gloop, and my personal favorite, Banana-Coco-Choco-Loco. Any prize from Peghiny's was a prize worth fighting for.

"It's hard to believe tomorrow's the big day," Jonathan said, looking around the classroom. Glue bottles, markers, scissors, scraps of construction paper, poster boards, and foam core displays littered the desks and floor.

Tomorrow.

It could spell the beginning of the end of my summer if things didn't go well. I had no crazy expectations about the judging. One group in our class, whose topic was fractions, was bringing in pizza to share. I also heard the division group was going to be using Hershey bars as part of their display. Our photographs were awesome, but how could we possibly compete with pizza and chocolate?

Jolina followed my gaze toward the fractions group.

"Everybody does pizza with fractions. And if they don't do pizza, they do apples or pie. It's way too predictable," she whispered. "They may have the math lesson down, but I doubt they'll score high creativity or originality points. Their display doesn't look much fun, anyway."

"I don't know," said Jonathan. "Free pizza? I mean, holy cow! That'll make fractions fun for anyone!"

Lucille giggled. "Don't you mean *whole-y* cow? Get it? *Whole-y*? As in *whole.*"

I gave Lucille a blank stare. Obviously I wasn't the only one affected by all the math.

Our display was a large tri-fold board of foam core into which I had poured all my creativity and energy. I had cut it to look like a giant tombstone and was meticulously gluing down letters to spell out MORTY'S MATH MEMORIAL across the top of the board. The twelve beautiful photos Aunt Willa had given us were lined up perfectly under the words. And under each photograph was the spreadsheet listing the animal's average life span in different time units ranging from seconds to years. I had to admit, it was kind of fun to discover that a Galapagos land tortoise lived, on average, 5,581,872,000 seconds.

The surprise prop Jolina brought was perfect. It was a stuffed opossum her mom found at the toy store. Jolina placed it on its back and arranged its paws to hold a small ball.

Lucille traced her finger around the edge of the board. "I'm so excited! I don't think I'm going to be able to sleep tonight. It's a good thing the math fair is first thing in the morning, or I'd go nuts waiting!"

"I know what you mean," I said, rubbing the glue from my hands. "Only I'm more nervous than excited. I mean, two test grades? That still freaks me out."

Jolina stood up the board. "You have to admit your feelings about math have changed a little, though, don't you think?"

"Yeah, a little, I guess. But that doesn't mean I don't worry about something as major as this. All my summer fun rides on this project!"

Jonathan picked up the stuffed opossum and tossed it back and forth in his hands. "If you're going to worry about something, Ella, worry about Harry. He's in the same group as Jimmy and Jean-Pierre and their topic is estimation. Last I heard, Jean-Pierre will be taking bets on the number of Triple-Fire Fireballs Harry can eat within a two-minute period—without throwing up, of course—and Jimmy is going to write everyone's estimations down. The student who's closest will get to take home a bag of Fireballs!"

We all turned to look at the daring Fireball trio. The title of their booth said it all: HARRY'S TRIPLE-

FIRE FIREBALL ESTIMATION EXTRAVAGANZA. The boys were huddled around their booth, leaning over a bowl as Jimmy dumped in bright red candy from a large bag. Harry took a piece, unwrapped it, and popped it into his mouth.

"What's he doing? Practicing?" Jolina asked.

I shrugged my shoulders and shook my head. "With Harry, you never really know."

CHAPTER TWENTY-ONE
HEIMLICH MANEUVER

Heim·lich ma·neu·ver
noun **hɪm**-lik mă-**noo**-věr\

—a first-aid procedure in which the abdomen of
a choking victim is pressed inward and upward
in order to assist in dislodging food or other
obstructions from the esophagus

E arly the next morning as I got ready for
school, Aunt Willa stopped me and gave me
a big hug.

"Your mom and dad and I will be at the awards ceremony. I want you to know I'm so proud of you, your team, and all the effort you've put into the math fair. No matter what happens, you should be proud of yourself."

She slid a small bag of gummy bears into my hand and winked. "Just in case you get hungry. I know they're your favorite."

"Thanks."

I ate a couple gummy bears on my way to school and shared some with Jolina and Lucille at the back gate. Then I shoved the rest in my pocket to save for later.

Inside the classroom, Ms. Carpenter clapped her hands to get our attention.

"Okay, listen up. We need to get started with the math fair. Teams, push your desks together so they form a table for your displays and props. Once your booth is set up, two members need to man it. The other members can walk around and look at the displays in our class and in the other fifth-grade classes as well. In an hour, team members need to switch places."

It took ten minutes for everyone to get set up. Lucille and I decided to take the first shift manning the booth. Jolina and Jonathan left to check out the other classes' projects.

Before long, we were hearing cries of "ahh . . . so cool" and "awesome" from kids visiting our booth. We had a box of paper, pencils, and calculators so students could figure out how old they were in the various time units. I figured out I was 5,765,760 minutes old at the time the math fair officially began. I also figured out I had to have the pencil stuck in my cast for 50,400 more minutes.

Right next to us, Jimmy and Jean-Pierre surveyed those who stopped by HARRY'S TRIPLE-FIRE FIREBALL ESTIMATION EXTRAVAGANZA and wrote down everyone's guesses. Lucille and I checked out their display when no one was visiting our booth and gave Jimmy our estimations. I think Harry was waiting for the judges to arrive before he actually started eating the candy.

About twenty minutes later, Mr. Morris and Mrs. Gottry began their judging. Armed with clipboards and pencils, they moved around the room, visiting with everyone and marking their score sheets. They stopped by the fractions booth and got slices of pizza, then went to division for a Hershey bar dessert. It would be a while until they reached us.

Ms. Carpenter had also started grading presentations and was making her way in our direction. My palms felt sweaty and I kept cracking my knuckles.

"Ella, stop that. There's nothing to be nervous about," Lucille said under her breath.

I shoved my hands in my pockets and discovered my bag of gummy bears. Lunch wasn't until after the awards ceremony and the smell of pizza was making me hungry. We weren't allowed to eat candy in class unless Ms. Carpenter had given it to us. But this technically wasn't class. It was the math fair. I logically concluded I could eat without breaking any rules (in theory). I grabbed a handful of the gummy bears and shoved them into my mouth.

Big mistake.

No sooner had I started to chew than Ms. Carpenter turned down the aisle toward our booth.

What if she didn't agree with my theory? What if she thought this *was* still class? I didn't want to get stuck with a detention when the school year was practically finished. I quickly tried to swallow the wad of gummy bears, but they had turned into a humongous slimy ball inside my mouth and got caught in my throat. My eyes widened with panic as I realized I couldn't breathe. I grabbed Lucille's arm, pointed to my throat, then put my hands around it in the choking sign.

"Oh no!" Lucille exclaimed. She rushed behind me, wrapped her arms around my stomach, and shoved her fists in and up, dislodging the globular mass of gummy bears.

I watched in horror as a slimy half-chewed confectionary cannonball soared through the air and splattered across our display.

"Ella, are you okay?" Lucille asked.

I felt absolutely mortified and just wanted to hide. As I stared at our display, my eyes widened. Globs of slobbery gelatin slid down the front, leaving multi-colored trails of saliva and sugar through the beautifully typed charts. Numbers became unreadable as they bled into each other.

Pieces of cherry, lemon, orange, and lime gummy bears had been spewed across Aunt Willa's beautiful photographs.

Right then and there, I gave up on my dream of a perfect score and thus a tutor-free summer. I had blown it, not only for myself, but for my whole team. Single-handedly, I'd managed to destroy our project.

I looked at Lucille and whispered, "I've ruined it."

"And you thought *I* would be the one to make it messy!" she said.

CHAPTER TWENTY-TWO

DISTRAUGHT

dis·traught

adjective \di-**strawt**\

—greatly upset with grief or worry

Lucille stared at our display as if in a trance. She seemed as shocked as I was at what just happened. Any points we would've scored for good craftsmanship and tidiness flew right out the window. Tears filled my eyes. I fought hard to keep them from falling down my cheeks, but some managed to escape anyway.

Ms. Carpenter must have seen what happened because I felt her hand on my shoulder. "Ella, sweetie, please don't cry. It will be okay. Really, it will. Let's get some paper towels, and I'm sure it will be fine," she whispered.

Lucille snapped out of her trance and went to grab a handful of paper towels. I gently blotted at the display board, trying to avoid smearing the ink even more, all the while feeling heavy with guilt. Lucille and Ms. Carpenter tidied up the table and picked up gummy globs that had fallen to the floor.

"Well, let's see what you've got here," said Mr. Morris, arriving at our board. He peered over his glasses and leaned in for a closer look. He quickly drew back. "Oh my."

"Gracious," Mrs. Gottry whispered. Even when she was shocked she still whispered.

Ms. Carpenter motioned Mr. Morris and Mrs. Gottry aside. They talked quietly to each other, nodded, and then moved on to HARRY'S TRIPLE-FIRE FIREBALL ESTIMATION EXTRAVAGANZA.

Ms. Carpenter wasn't making a big deal out of my catastrophic candy mishap and the destruction of our display. This made me believe she was the world's best teacher. I felt embarrassed enough already without the whole class turning their attention our way.

Ms. Carpenter stepped back and looked over our display. "Well," she paused. "It doesn't look *that* bad."

"It doesn't look bad," I said. "It looks terrible!"

Ms. Carpenter opened her mouth to say something, but just then Jimmy shouted, "Watch out! He's gonna blow!"

We turned around in time to see Harry, his face bright pink, spewing bits of chewed up Fireballs high into the air. He looked like an erupting human volcano. Mrs. Gottry took cover behind Mr. Morris, and Mr. Morris took cover behind his clipboard as small Fireball pieces rained down.

Ms. Carpenter cried out in horror, grabbed the trashcan, and shoved it into Harry's arms. He bent his head over the can and threw up the rest of the Triple-Fire Fireballs.

"You never learn, do you, Harry?" Ms. Carpenter sighed. She patted him on the back and asked Jimmy to grab him a cup of water.

"This probably disqualifies us from the Best of Show award, doesn't it?" Jimmy asked.

Mr. Morris and Mrs. Gottry nodded, but I could see Mr. Morris's shoulders shaking as though he were trying hard not to laugh.

Between Harry's human volcano and my giant gummy bear loogie, there was more food flying through the air than during a cafeteria food fight.

Brushing bits of sticky candy from his clipboard, Mr. Morris and Mrs. Gottry left to judge the booths in the other classes. "See you at the awards ceremony," Mr. Morris said to Ms. Carpenter on his way out the door.

"We can't wait," Ms. Carpenter said excitedly.

It didn't seem right that my teacher was so happy when just moments earlier I had sealed the deal for my team to get a lousy math grade. With all the damage done, I didn't see how Ms. Carpenter would be able to grade it. I glanced at Lucille. She still looked pretty upset. What was I supposed to say to her? Somehow "sorry" didn't seem like enough.

When Jonathan and Jolina returned to take their turn manning our booth, their jaws dropped.

"What happened?" Jolina squawked.

Before I could explain, Harry came up behind me, draped an arm over my shoulder, and said, "Oh man, you should've seen it! It was awesome. Stuff was flying everywhere."

"You should talk!" I replied angrily, shrugging his arm off my shoulder.

He looked at me and smiled. It wasn't a mean smile, just a dorky, amused one. He actually thought this whole thing was funny! That it was entertaining! I couldn't believe it. I glared at him and walked away from the whole group. I wanted to be alone and have a good cry. I went where I always did for a sob session—the girls' bathroom.

CHAPTER TWENTY-THREE

CLIFFHANGER

cliff·hang·er

noun **klif**-hang-ĕr\

—a contest whose outcome is in doubt up
to the very end

T he way I saw it, I had ruined my chances of a fun-filled summer and had also humiliated myself in front of everyone. But worse was the fact my friends would probably never speak to me again. It wasn't just me who would get a failing grade for the math fair; they would, too.

The bathroom door opened. I looked up from my seat on the floor to see Jolina and Lucille come in.

"How'd you know I was here?" I asked, sniffling and trying to control my quivering chin.

"Lucky guess, I suppose," Lucille said. "We're not mad at you, Ella. It was an accident."

"But . . . I . . . made . . . a . . . complete mess of . . . it," I spluttered, tears streaming down my face.

"True, but Mr. Morris and Mrs. Gottry had already judged it, right?" said Jolina.

I bit my lip as I exchanged glances with Lucille. Lucille shook her head.

Jolina sagged against a bathroom stall door. "Oh man," she moaned.

"And what's worse, Ms. Carpenter hadn't graded it yet either—and now she can't. The numbers, the charts—everything—it's all smeared. It's ruined and there's no time to redo it. It's worth two tests, remember? We're going to get a zero!" I wailed.

I had just sabotaged Jolina's straight-A track record.

Lucille placed her hands on her hips and looked me in the eyes. "If we all work together, we can do it. There's still the foam core board I brought in earlier this week. Everyone can print out a new list of time conversions for their animals. You'll need to get a different photo of a platypus to replace the ruined one—it won't be as nice as your aunt's photo but it will work. Jolina and Jonathan can get other pictures of the lion and boa constrictor, and we can reuse the ones that aren't ruined." She squatted down and gently touched my shoulder. "Ella, there isn't time to make it *perfect* again, but there is time to make it *good.*"

She was right. My way of doing things obviously hadn't worked out for me—from insisting turtles didn't live long to demanding the project had to be perfect, hurting Lucille's feelings in the process.

By redoing it, I might stand a small chance of at least getting a passing grade for the project. And though I doubted it would be enough to save my summer from being toast, at least my friends wouldn't fail because of me.

Lucille smiled and stood. "Splash some water on your face, blow your nose, and come out of the bathroom. Jolina, Jonathan, and I will talk to Ms. Carpenter to see if we can have a few extra minutes to pull stuff together."

I sniffed and nodded and picked myself up off the floor. And even though I wasn't done feeling sorry for myself, I cleaned up and headed back to the classroom.

I could see my three teammates talking with Ms. Carpenter. They raced over seconds later.

"C'mon—she can give us forty-five minutes, but after that the fair's over and everyone will have to go to the awards ceremony," Lucille said.

Since Mrs. Gottry was a judge, she had locked the library, so we couldn't use the computers there. We decided to split up to go to different classrooms.

"Let's meet back in our class in twenty minutes," Lucille said.

Because we were on different computers, we all came back with different fonts and layouts on our spreadsheets. While Lucille glued down the new title, Jolina, Jonathan, and I matched the animal photos with the right spreadsheets. Jonathan didn't know to print his photos in color, so they were in black and white. The printer I used ran out of colored ink halfway through my print job, so the platypus came out colored like a rainbow. As soon as we had one animal grouped with its spreadsheet, we handed it to Lucille, who squirted it with glue and slapped it down on the foam core. Every once in a while, I'd look up and see Ms. Carpenter watching us.

"Done!" said Lucille, standing up the board. Glue dripped down from most of the photos, two of the spreadsheets were crooked, and MORTY'S MATH MEMORYAL was misspelled. And surprisingly enough, it didn't bother me—Lucille was proud of her work, and it was because of her that we even got it done. It wasn't perfect, or even close to it, but maybe it was enough to help my friends, even if it was too late for me.

Jolina looked at the classroom clock. "We finished with five minutes to spare." She exhaled loudly. "Why don't you and Lucille walk around now since you haven't had a chance to see the other displays yet? Jonathan and I will take this over to our table and show Ms. Carpenter. Mr. Morris and Mrs. Gottry won't be able to judge it, but at least Ms. Carpenter can grade it."

Lucille and I wandered around until Mr. Morris's voice came over the loud speaker telling everyone it was time to get ready for the awards ceremony.

CHAPTER TWENTY-FOUR
CRESTFALLEN

crest·fall·en

noun **krest**-faw-lĕn/

—downcast, disappointed at failure

I scanned the auditorium, looking for Aunt Willa and my parents. I wished now they hadn't planned to come. What would I say to Aunt Willa about what happened to her beautiful photographs? How was I going to tell my parents I'd be failing math because I upchucked a bunch of gummy bears on our project?

I spotted them up ahead and gasped. Apparently I wouldn't have to tell them—Ms. Carpenter was doing it for me. My dad slowly shook his head and my mom frowned. I sighed as I shuffled down the aisle with my classmates. Glancing back over my shoulder, I saw Ms. Carpenter hand Mom a sheet of paper and shake hands with Aunt Willa. No doubt the sheet of paper was a list of math tutors my parents could hire over the summer. Then Ms. Carpenter took a seat at the end of our row. I slumped in my chair and, wallowing in self-pity, looked at the stage where Mr. Morris and Mrs. Gottry stood.

Next to the podium was a long table holding lots of ribbons and the coveted trophies—and we'd get none of them. If only our project had been judged *before* my gummy bear spew. If we had won a ribbon, Ms. Carpenter would have known it was worthy of an A. If a project was ribbon-worthy, it must be A-worthy, too, right? It didn't matter, though—I was toast.

Mr. Morris stepped up to the microphone. "Before we hand out awards, I want to let everyone know Mrs. Gottry and I had a wonderful time at the first ever Victor Waldo Elementary Math Fair! We had a very difficult time choosing the winners, particularly the Best of Show. Everyone did an excellent job. We are proud of all of you."

It was your typical speech—the kind adults feel they need to make so nobody's feelings get hurt. By all the muted groans, I could tell my classmates just wanted to know who was going to get a ribbon or a trophy, not to mention the Peghiny's Ice Cream Sundaes. There were six classes competing, so there were a lot of ribbons to hand out.

Our class was the last to have the winners announced. Mr. Morris started with third place. "Despite some mishaps, third place goes to Harry, Jimmy, and Jean-Pierre! They had a rather, uh, unique approach to estimating and showed a true understanding of the skill. Congratulations to the three of you."

Everyone clapped (except for me). I was still mad at Harry for thinking my blow out with the gummy bears was funny.

Mr. Morris took up the second-place ribbon. "Second place goes to Lucas, Ernesto, and Deion for the excellent Hershey bar review of division. What a topic! Very well done, boys."

There were only the first place ribbons left. I didn't care about who won. I knew then it wasn't us.

"First place goes to Rashawna, Sarah, and Alejandra for their display on fractions. Great job with the pizza, young ladies."

Mr. Morris said more stuff about what a great job everyone did, but I barely heard him. It was Aunt Willa's horrendously loud wolf whistle and cheering from the back of the auditorium that snapped me out of my trance.

"Wait. What happened?" I said.

"C'mon! We just won Best of Show!" Lucille grabbed my arm and dragged me down our aisle.

I tripped over a backpack. "We did? How?"

"I don't know!" she squealed.

Jonathan and Jolina slapped us high-fives as Lucille and I joined them on stage. Mr. Morris shook our hands as he handed each of us a small golden trophy with a person holding a star above his head. "You four had the most original approach to time conversions we've ever seen!"

"Thanks," Jolina said.

Lucille admired her trophy. "It was Jonathan's idea."

"Yeah, but we couldn't have done it without Morty," Jonathan said.

"Or Lucille," I said, quietly.

She smiled back at me.

Mr. Morris turned back to the microphone. "This group, we felt, showed a true grasp of their topic and also chose to share it in a way that was original. I am sure they are surprised, more than anybody, to find themselves up here since their project suffered an odd tragedy that prevented it from being judged. It was the spirit of true teamwork they showed, while working under a great deal of pressure, that prompted their teacher to invite us back for a second look. Once again, great job to everyone!"

We had our picture taken with Mr. Morris and Mrs. Gottry, and he dismissed the audience to go to lunch.

I walked down the stage stairs and raced back to my seat to grab my backpack. I needed to talk to Ms. Carpenter about my grade right away. Without a doubt, I knew she would give us an A now.

I pushed and shoved my way back to my seat. I could see my family, along with Ms. Carpenter, fighting their way down the main aisle, through a sea of students, toward the front of the auditorium.

I slung my backpack over my shoulder and decided it'd be easier just to meet them halfway. I climbed over a couple rows of chairs when my trophy fell from my back pack. I dropped my bag and got on my hands and knees to find it, hoping it didn't break. I searched around candy wrappers, torn up papers, and chewed gum. Eventually, my fingertips grazed the marble base of the trophy.

The noise level had dropped while I was looking for my trophy. Most of my classmates had left, it seemed. A familiar voice drifted down from the center aisle.

"I just thought you might want to know ahead of time. That way you can be the ones to give her the news about her grade." I cocked my head—that was Ms. Carpenter's voice.

That didn't sound good. I felt sorry for whomever Ms. Carpenter was talking about.

"Thanks. We appreciate the heads up."

Wait a minute—that was my dad's voice!

I stood up with a jolt, my trophy clutched in my hand. "Hold on," I said, my voice quivering. "We just won Best of Show and I *still* failed math and have to have a tutor? That's not fair. We worked so hard and now you're saying it was all for nothing!"

All four of them stared at me with their mouth open.

"What on earth were you doing on the floor?" Mom said.

"I dropped my trophy . . . which apparently isn't worth much if I still didn't pass math."

"Oh no, honey. That's not at all what Ms. Carpenter was saying." Mom whisked down the row and hugged me. "You think you failed math?"

I buried my head in Mom's arms and cried for the third time that day.

"No—actually, Ms. Carpenter was telling us that you did extremely well. In fact, with your last pop quiz and this project, you pulled your grade up to a low B."

I snapped my head up and wiped my eyes. "I got a B?"

Mom nodded.

"In math?"

All four of them laughed.

I peeked around Mom to see Ms. Carpenter. I could feel my face turning red. "I heard you say something to them about breaking news to me—it sounded bad." I mumbled.

She nodded. "I knew that there was the possibility that you might get tutored over the summer because of your math grade. I wanted them to be able to tell you the good news in a special way since you have worked so hard."

"But I don't understand. Our project was dripping with glue, the fonts didn't match, the platypus looked like a confused chameleon, and words were misspelled. How is it possible that we got a good grade?"

Ms. Carpenter gently shook her head. "Ella, your team got an A because I saw how hard everyone worked and your willingness to keep on trying until the very end. Yes, craftsmanship is important, but I know your first project was beautiful. I wasn't going to punish your team for an accident." She winked. "And, of course, your math was correct, too."

"That's my Ella-vator," Dad said with a wink.

"What was that piece of paper you handed Mom?" I asked.

Ms. Carpenter laughed again. "It was just a recipe she had asked for weeks ago. I kept forgetting to send it home with you and when I saw her here today, I ran back to the classroom to get it."

"Oh." I looked at my feet. "I thought it was a list of tutors."

"Ella Bella," Aunt Willa said, "you're something else."

CHAPTER TWENTY-FIVE

RECONCILE

rec·on·cile

verb **rek**-ŏn-sɪl\

—to restore a relationship after a quarrel

"This really is the best ice cream in the world," I declared, digging my spoon into my sundae. "How can you possibly go wrong with Banana-Coco-Choco-Loco?"

Between Jonathan, Lucille, Jolina, me, and all our siblings and parents, we took up most of the seating in Peghiny's Ice Cream Parlor. It was like having our own private celebration.

"I don't know about that, Ella. I'm not a big coconut fan," said Jonathan, wrinkling his nose. "But the Soda Pop Sundae Swirl rocks big time!"

I stuck out my tongue and made a funny face. He laughed and stuck his tongue out in reply. Across the table, Lucille alternated between stirring her ice cream into a mushy mess and licking the spoon. Jolina sat next to her, enjoying her strawberry shake instead of a sundae. Our four shiny trophies, along with the stuffed opossum, were arranged in the middle of our table. It was the strangest centerpiece I'd ever seen.

"I still can't believe they went back and judged our project," Jonathan said.

Jolina nodded. "I know. When they called our names up on stage, I thought I'd gone crazy and was hearing things."

"I'm still amazed that even with all the mismatched fonts, multi-colored animals, dripping glue, and bad spelling, they gave us Best of Show," said Lucille.

I looked at Lucille. "It was a math project, not a spelling test."

"Well, look who's not a perfectionist anymore," she said, winking.

I swallowed a big blob of ice cream and gave myself some major brain freeze. Someone once told me if I pressed my thumb on the roof of my mouth, brain freeze would go away fast.

"Bwan fweez," I said, with my thumb in my mouth.

All three of them nodded.

Aunt Willa came over with her camera. "Let's have a victory photo with your ice cream. Everybody lean in."

She took a couple different shots and then headed back to the grown-ups' table. I thought of the animal photographs she had taken and how *I* was the one who destroyed them because I didn't follow Ms. Carpenter's rules about candy in the classroom. It was kind of the same situation with Aunt Willa—only reversed. I had a set of rules I wanted her to follow; the only difference was I never *told* her my rules. I didn't tell her anything until after I blew up at her. True, some of the fault was hers, but I was beginning to realize that I wasn't completely innocent either. I knew I owed her an apology . . . a real one this time.

"Hey, Aunt Willa," I said and squeezed out of the booth, pulling her over to the stools at the counter.

"What's up, Ella Bella?"

I stared down at my feet and took a deep breath. "I'm sorry I yelled at you."

"You said that already," Aunt Willa said.

"I know," I whispered. My chest felt tight. "But this time I actually mean it."

Aunt Willa smiled while she swiveled back and forth on her stool. "Ah. Are you saying that earlier I got the 'my-mother's-standing-right-here-what-else-am-I-going-to-say' apology?"

I blushed. "Yes."

"I knew that was the version I was getting at the time. But I was willing to take what I could get."

"It's not really your fault about the candle and the panpipe music. I never told you. I also never told you how crazy organized I have to have things. I didn't want to hurt your feelings, but I guess I ended up doing that anyway when I exploded at you."

She gave me a big hug. "I promise not to play my music or light smelly candles when you're in the room. And I won't touch your stuff without talking to you first. Deal?"

I nodded. "Deal. And I promise if something's bothering me, I'll talk to you right away and not erupt like a volcano." I bit my lip. "I also promise not to chase Chewy."

She laughed. "You and Chewy can shake on that when we get home."

As I slid back in the booth, Lucille asked, "What was that all about?"

"Just something I needed to say to my room-mate."

"How is it sharing a room with your aunt?"

"Let's just say it's getting better," I said with a smile.

CHAPTER TWENTY-SIX
PROPOSITION

prop·o·si·tion
noun \prop-ŏ-**zish**-ŏn\

—a problem or undertaking, something
to be dealt with

That night after dinner, Jolina, Lucille, and Jonathan stopped by my house. We all grabbed sodas and went to my room.

"Sit down, Ella," Jolina said. "There's something we need to talk to you about."

I plopped on my bed and looked at the three of them. "What's up?"

Jolina took a deep breath. "Mrs. Peghiny has a proposition for us."

I leaned forward. "The ice cream parlor owner? She has a what?"

"A population," Lucille said.

Jolina shook her head. "No, Lucille, a proposition. It means an offer. Every July Fourth, Mrs. Peghiny introduces a new flavor—something that's unique, that only Peghiny's has."

"The problem is," Jonathan said, "she says she's just not sure what flavor to invent next—she needs some market research done. She called it 'statistical analysis.' And she thinks *we're* the perfect people to help."

Jolina sat down next to me. "She wants us to survey our classmates and neighbors to find out what flavors they want."

"And as payment for our statistical analysis," interrupted Lucille, "we can name the new flavor. *And* she'll give us each a free ice cream cone every week for the whole summer."

"That's twelve weeks times four of us . . . forty-eight ice cream cones!" Jonathan exclaimed.

"Hold your horses, let me get this straight." I set down my soda. "This is math, right?" I asked them suspiciously.

"Yes, Ella, it's math," said Jonathan.

A flash of lightning suddenly lit up the outside, followed closely by a tremendous boom of thunder. Sheets of rain poured down. I rolled my eyes, shook my head, and sighed.

"Wow! Look at that rain. Came out of nowhere, didn't it?" Lucille said.

Jolina squeezed my shoulder. "Ella, it's math but with ice cream! I say we do it. We can do surveys, graphing, and come up with some percentages. What does everyone think? Are we in?"

"I'm totally in," Jonathan said.

"Me, too!" said Lucille.

All eyes were on me. "The whole point of scoring well on the math fair was so I could *avoid* doing math over the summer. Now, because we did a good job, I'm going to have to do *more* math?"

"Don't look at it as doing more math," Jonathan said. "Look at it as eating more ice cream."

I *was* supposed to be working on my attitude toward math, after all.

Another crack of thunder sounded as lightning lit up the sky. The last storm hadn't brought the bad luck I thought it would. Not in the end, anyway.

"Well," I mumbled. "I guess I'm in. It *is* ice cream."

I stared out the window. Another rainstorm. Another math project.

I heard Aunt Willa down the hall laughing with my parents. In my mind, I could hear her voice: *just because you don't like something doesn't mean you can ignore it and hope it goes away.*

I looked at my friends. We made a good team, and with their help, I was sure we could do the work needed to get those free ice cream cones all summer.

"Bring it on," I said and smiled.

MORTY'S MATH MEMORIAL

Black Widow: 1 year or . . .

$\dfrac{1\ \cancel{\text{year}}}{1} \times \dfrac{12\ \text{months}}{1\ \cancel{\text{year}}} = 12\ \text{months}$

$\dfrac{1\ \cancel{\text{year}}}{1} \times \dfrac{52\ \text{weeks}}{1\ \cancel{\text{year}}} = 52\ \text{weeks}$

$\dfrac{1\ \cancel{\text{year}}}{1} \times \dfrac{365\ \text{days}}{1\ \cancel{\text{year}}} = 365\ \text{days}$

$\dfrac{365\ \cancel{\text{days}}}{1} \times \dfrac{24\ \text{hours}}{1\ \cancel{\text{day}}} = 8{,}760\ \text{hours}$

$\dfrac{8{,}760\ \cancel{\text{hours}}}{1} \times \dfrac{60\ \text{minutes}}{1\ \cancel{\text{hour}}} = 525{,}600\ \text{minutes}$

$\dfrac{525{,}600\ \cancel{\text{minutes}}}{1} \times \dfrac{60\ \text{seconds}}{1\ \cancel{\text{minute}}} = 31{,}536{,}000\ \text{seconds}$

Opossum: 2 years or . . .

$\underline{\text{2 years}}$ x $\underline{\text{12 months}}$ = 24 months
  1   1 year

$\underline{\text{2 years}}$ x $\underline{\text{52 weeks}}$ = 104 weeks
  1   1 year

$\underline{\text{2 years}}$ x $\underline{\text{365 days}}$ = 730 days
  1   1 year

$\underline{\text{730 days}}$ x $\underline{\text{24 hours}}$ = 17,520 hours
  1   1 day

$\underline{\text{17,520 hours}}$ x $\underline{\text{60 minutes}}$ = 1,051,200 minutes
  1   1 hour

$\underline{\text{1,051,200 minutes}}$ x $\underline{\text{60 seconds}}$ = 63,072,000 seconds
  1   1 minute

Porcupine: 6 years or . . .

$\underline{\text{6 years}}$ x $\underline{\text{12 months}}$ = 72 months
  1   1 year

$\underline{\text{6 years}}$ x $\underline{\text{52 weeks}}$ = 312 weeks
  1   1 year

$\underline{\text{6 years}}$ x $\underline{\text{365 days}}$ = 2,190 days
  1   1 year

$\underline{\text{2,190 days}}$ x $\underline{\text{24 hours}}$ = 52,560 hours
  1   1 day

$\underline{\text{52,560 hours}}$ x $\underline{\text{60 minutes}}$ =3,153,600 minutes
    1   1 hour

$\underline{\text{3,153,600 minutes}}$ x $\underline{\text{60 seconds}}$ = 189,216,000 seconds
    1   1 minute

Giraffe: 10 years or . . .

10 ~~years~~ x 12 months = 120 months
  1   1 ~~year~~

10 ~~years~~ x 52 weeks = 520 weeks
  1   1 ~~year~~

10 ~~years~~ x 365 days = 3,650 days
  1   1 ~~year~~

3,650 ~~days~~ x 24 hours = 87,600 hours
  1   1 ~~day~~

87,600 ~~hours~~ x 60 minutes = 5,256,000 minutes
  1   1 ~~hour~~

5,256,000 ~~minutes~~ x 60 seconds =315,360,000 seconds
  1   1 ~~minute~~

Platypus: 12 years or . . .

12 ~~years~~ x 12 months = 144 months
  1   1 ~~year~~

12 ~~years~~ x 52 weeks = 624 weeks
  1   1 ~~year~~

12 ~~years~~ x 365 days = 4,380 days
  1   1 ~~year~~

4,380 ~~days~~ x 24 hours = 105,120 hours
  1   1 ~~day~~

105,120 ~~hours~~ x 60 minutes = 6,307,200 minutes
  1   1 ~~hour~~

6,307,200 ~~minutes~~ x 60 seconds =378,432,000 seconds
  1   1 ~~minute~~

African Lion: 15 years or . . .

$\underline{\text{15 years}}$ x $\underline{\text{12 months}}$ = 180 months
  1   1 year

$\underline{\text{15 years}}$ x $\underline{\text{52 weeks}}$ = 780 weeks
  1   1 year

$\underline{\text{15 years}}$ x $\underline{\text{365 days}}$ = 5,475 days
  1   1 year

$\underline{\text{5,475 days}}$ x $\underline{\text{24 hours}}$ = 131,400 hours
  1   1 day

$\underline{\text{131,400 hours}}$ x $\underline{\text{60 minutes}}$ = 7,884,000 minutes
  1   1 hour

$\underline{\text{7,884,000 minutes}}$ x $\underline{\text{60 seconds}}$ = 473,040,000 seconds
      1   1 minute

Boa Constrictor: 20 years or . . .

$\underline{\text{20 years}}$ x $\underline{\text{12 months}}$ = 240 months
  1   1 year

$\underline{\text{20 years}}$ x $\underline{\text{52 weeks}}$ = 1,040 weeks
  1   1 year

$\underline{\text{20 years}}$ x $\underline{\text{365 days}}$ = 7,300 days
  1   1 year

$\underline{\text{7,300 days}}$ x $\underline{\text{24 hours}}$ = 175,200 hours
  1   1 day

$\underline{\text{175,200 hours}}$ x $\underline{\text{60 minutes}}$ = 10,512,000 minutes
  1   1 hour

$\underline{\text{10,512,000 minutes}}$ x $\underline{\text{60 seconds}}$ =630,720,000 seconds
      1   1 minute

Hippopotamus: 40 years or . . .

$$\frac{40 \text{ years}}{1} \times \frac{12 \text{ months}}{1 \text{ year}} = 480 \text{ months}$$

$$\frac{40 \text{ years}}{1} \times \frac{52 \text{ weeks}}{1 \text{ year}} = 2{,}080 \text{ weeks}$$

$$\frac{40 \text{ years}}{1} \times \frac{365 \text{ days}}{1 \text{ year}} = 14{,}600 \text{ days}$$

$$\frac{14{,}600 \text{ days}}{1} \times \frac{24 \text{ hours}}{1 \text{ day}} = 350{,}400 \text{ hours}$$

$$\frac{350{,}400 \text{ hours}}{1} \times \frac{60 \text{ minutes}}{1 \text{ hour}} = 21{,}024{,}000 \text{ minutes}$$

$$\frac{21{,}024{,}000 \text{ minutes}}{1} \times \frac{60 \text{ seconds}}{1 \text{ minute}} = 1{,}261{,}440{,}000 \text{ seconds}$$

Arabian Camel: 50 years or . . .

$$\frac{50 \text{ years}}{1} \times \frac{12 \text{ months}}{1 \text{ year}} = 600 \text{ months}$$

$$\frac{50 \text{ years}}{1} \times \frac{52 \text{ weeks}}{1 \text{ year}} = 2{,}600 \text{ weeks}$$

$$\frac{50 \text{ years}}{1} \times \frac{365 \text{ days}}{1 \text{ year}} = 18{,}250 \text{ days}$$

$$\frac{18{,}250 \text{ days}}{1} \times \frac{24 \text{ hours}}{1 \text{ day}} = 438{,}000 \text{ hours}$$

$$\frac{438{,}000 \text{ hours}}{1} \times \frac{60 \text{ minutes}}{1 \text{ hour}} = 26{,}280{,}000 \text{ minutes}$$

$$\frac{26{,}280{,}000 \text{ minutes}}{1} \times \frac{60 \text{ seconds}}{1 \text{ minute}} = 1{,}576{,}800{,}000 \text{ seconds}$$

African Elephant: 70 years or . . .

70 ~~years~~ x 12 months = 840 months
  1   1 ~~year~~

70 ~~years~~ x 52 weeks = 3,640 weeks
  1   1 ~~year~~

70 ~~years~~ x 365 days = 25,550 days
  1   1 ~~year~~

25,550 ~~days~~ x 24 hours = 613,200 hours
  1   1 ~~day~~

613,200 ~~hours~~ x 60 minutes = 36,792,000 minutes
  1   1 ~~hour~~

36,792,000 ~~minutes~~ x 60 seconds = 2,207,520,000 seconds
  1   1 ~~minute~~

Box Turtle: 100 years or . . .

100 ~~years~~ x 12 months = 1,200 months
  1   1 ~~year~~

100 ~~years~~ x 52 weeks = 5,200 weeks
  1   1 ~~year~~

100 ~~years~~ x 365 days = 36,500 days
  1   1 ~~year~~

36,500 ~~days~~ x 24 hours = 876,000 hours
  1   1 ~~day~~

876,000 ~~hours~~ x 60 minutes =52,560,000 minutes
  1   1 ~~hour~~

52,560,000 ~~minutes~~ x 60 seconds = 3,153,600,000 seconds
  1   1 ~~minute~~

Galapagos Land Tortoise: 177 years or . . .

177 ~~years~~ x 12 months = 2,124 months
  1   1 ~~year~~

177 ~~years~~ x 52 weeks = 9,204 weeks
  1   1 ~~year~~

177 ~~years~~ x 365 days = 64,605 days
  1   1 ~~year~~

64,605 ~~days~~ x 24 hours = 1,550,520 hours
  1   1 ~~day~~

1,550,520 ~~hours~~ x 60 minutes = 93,031,200 minutes
    1   1 ~~hour~~

93,031,200 ~~minutes~~ x 60 seconds = 5,581,872,000 seconds
    1   1 ~~minute~~

Lifespans found at:
- http://animaldiversity.ummz.umich.edu
- www.nationalgeographic.com
- http://opossumsocietyus.org
- www.pittsburghzoo.org
- www.wildlife.org.au

ACKNOWLEDGMENTS

A special thanks to my husband, David, for drinking tea on the front porch while reading and editing my story, all because he loves me . . . and because I didn't mention him in my first book . . . and he's never let me forget it!

Thank you to my fellow SCBWI Inkstigators and also to Word Weavers—for your thoughtful critiques and words of encouragement.

J SOUDERS
Souders, Taryn,
Dead possums are fair game /
R2004892929 EAST_A

Atlanta-Fulton Public Library